CALL MAMA

CALL MAMA

TERRY H. WATSON

Matador
9 Priory Business Park,
Wistow Road, Kibworth Beauchamp,
Leicestershire. LE8 0RX
Tel: (+44) 116 279 2299
Fax: (+44) 116 279 2277
Email: books@troubador.co.uk
Web: www.troubador.co.uk/matador

ISBN 978 1784623 500

British Library Cataloguing in Publication Data.
A catalogue record for this book is available from the British Library.

Typeset by Troubador Publishing Ltd, Leicester, UK

Matador is an imprint of Troubador Publishing Ltd

For Drew
My husband, my soul mate, my best friend.

ACKNOWLEDGEMENTS

My sincere thanks to the following people who helped *Call Mama* along the way.

Rebecca Forster, USA Today & Amazon Bestselling Author, who inspired me to write, encouraged and advised me.

My proofreaders Susan O'Donnell and Marie Condron, both of whom edited with honesty and clarity.

Jonathan McGuinness and my beautiful and talented great-niece Emma Archondakis, for their assistance and suggestions for the cover.

Family and friends for support and heartening good wishes for the success of *Call Mama* and finally, Drew, my rock.

Enjoy the read!

CHAPTER 1

"I'm not going on the bus," lamented the girl. Her cry went unheard in the howling wind cutting through the depressing bus depot with missing windows, broken seats and a filthy wet floor that increased in danger with the entrance of each passenger. The relentless wind whipped the icy snow into a frenzy, as passengers huddled closer together, the luckier ones being out of direct blast of the blizzard.

"I'm not going on the bus," mumbled the girl to no one in particular.

A bus arrived, transported the girl and her travelling companion seven miles or so from South Halsted to Wentworth where they waited for a long-haul bus to arrive. Much later than scheduled, the bus emerged from the dimness and slithered to a halt outside the shelter. The driver announced his destination, checked tickets and boarding proceeded.

"No heating!" proclaimed the driver, an unnecessary comment as, one by one, passengers took their seats in the icebox container that was to transport them overnight, several hundred miles further from the rawness of the Chicago winter.

"Take it or leave it, folks. The company won't send another vehicle out tonight. It might kick in as we go along," he said none too convincingly.

The girl huddled into her jacket, shivering and

miserable beside the man who appeared to be her minder, similarly cold and dreary as he contemplated the task ahead. The journey continued, wipers fighting a losing battle as the storm increased in intensity and ferocity.

A fat man, occupying two seats, began to snore, reaching a crescendo in time to the battering elements attacking the cold window where his head rested. Some weary hours later, the driver announced a stop. Relieved passengers headed for the warmth and comfort of a diner. Had she wanted to leave the confines of her situation, the girl would have nowhere to run, no one to run to and no one to care about her traumatized state. No one noticed the troubled girl in seat eight.

The fat man slept through the comfort break. Passengers returning to their seats were treated to the rise and fall of the snoring concerto. Some found it amusing.

In spite of the bitter cold, the girl slept. Further comfort stops took place. With a change of drivers, Bob, the new person, introduced himself and adjusted the heating, which for the remainder of the long journey emitted some form of heat. Throughout most of the thirteen or so hours, the girl slept fitfully until nudged awake by the slowing of the engine and activity of passengers gathering their belongings in anticipation of an escape from the chilly tomb of the bus.

The girl and her companion walked tentatively for some time along an icy pathway towards their destination: a rundown house, one of many in a nondescript inner city street of New York. A middle aged woman opened the door to them and studied the girl sternly before admitting her to the relative warmth of the house.

The man remained at the door and uttered a curt command.

"Keep her until you are given further instructions."

He handed her a vial. "Use as instructed, one drop morning and evening in a drink."

With that, he departed into the cold of the night.

Inside, the woman escorted the girl to a cosy kitchen, sat her down and served soup, which she devoured in moments. She was too traumatized to ask for more. Warmed by the food and fighting to stay awake, she allowed her host to escort her to a sofa where she slept soundly.

✻

It was mid-morning before the mother knew her daughter was missing. A frantic call to her office from her housekeeper alerted her to her child's absence from home and set alarm bells ringing. Soon, local police officers, satisfied that it was out of character for the girl not to be where expected and given the mother's high profile in the community, set in motion a search that was to take them out of their Chicago zone to the much wider realm of distant states.

✻

Several days later and with no sign of the storm abating, the woman received a package containing a change of clothes for the girl, clothes obviously chosen with care and perfect in size, which any young girl in perhaps a different situation would be proud to wear. Along with the package came instructions to "have the kid ready for collection in eight hours". She had orders to incinerate her old clothes, making sure no trace remained on the premises.

Bathed and changed, the girl, still drugged from regular sleeping draughts, was transferred from the supervision of her sitter back to the care of her bus companion, who escorted her a short walk. As pre-arranged, he left her at a phone booth, instructing her not to move, not that she was capable of moving far. Once he was out of sight, a woman arrived and bundled her into a campervan, which sped off into the night. The woman administered a mild sedative, laid the girl on a bed and covered her with a duvet. Had she been more *compos mentis*, the girl would perhaps have appreciated the standard of her surroundings, coming as she did from the luxurious life that she shared with her mother and household staff, whom she adored. The only sound she could utter was something sounding like "Call Mama".

The vehicle travelled on at speed, passing through Pennsylvania and entering Ohio some three hundred miles later. Strong winds, falling temperatures and scattered snow showers made driving difficult. Listening to the radio report, the travellers learned of an impending snowstorm.

"It's no use attempting to go further tonight. Even with these winter tyres the van is slipping dangerously. We will hole up at the next motel. I have to call Boss."

On the outskirts of Cleveland, two people registered at a motel. No one witnessed a bundle wrapped in a duvet being carried to the room. The trio remained there for three days until it was deemed safe enough to continue their journey.

Her two minders took it in turn to drive and to see to their captive, administering to her every need with a tenderness and concern that contradicted the heinousness of their crime. They continued to administer small drops of mild sedative to keep her calm.

The sedative had first been given to her after school,

when a member of her mother's staff collected her. She had expected someone else to meet her but accepted without question the explanation of an emergency dental appointment, remembering that the family helper had complained of toothache. She climbed into the back of the car and handed over her cello case for safe-keeping. She was unaware of the prick of a sharp needle as it jabbed her arm.

"Sorry," whispered the man. "I hate to do this." He picked up her mobile phone, sent a text and removed the SIM card, which he then destroyed.

CHAPTER 2

In her tastefully furnished sitting room in her Lincoln Park home, Brenda Mears constantly dabbed her eyes as Detective Tony Harvey, Chief of the Bureau of Detectives of the Chicago Police Department, and Detective Carole Carr, his deputy chief, enquired about her daughter's disappearance, probing gently to establish facts about the incident that they had come to investigate.

"So, Lucy was to spend the night at a friend's house?"

"Yes. They were to go for pizza and see a movie. Lucy had arranged to sleep over with Abigail. Gina, Abigail's mom, had arranged to drop her off here after lunch in time for her cello lesson with Ken Farmer."

"Where did she have her lessons?" asked Detective Carr.

"Here, in our music room on the first floor. Ken has been coming to the house since Lucy was nine years old."

"Tell me again, Brenda," said Detective Harvey. "We know Lucy didn't spend the night at Abigail's, did she?"

Brenda sobbed quietly. "So I believe. Abigail had a text from Lucy saying she would take a rain check as she was sick."

"Lucy's phone has not been found," continued Harvey. "We have established the text did come from her number and from the vicinity of school. What bothers me is why Lucy didn't speak directly to Abigail before school finished."

"I don't know! I don't know!" wailed the distraught mother, collapsing in a flood of uncontrollable tears. "Please, please, find my daughter."

Carr, herself a mother, tried to comfort the distraught woman.

"We'll do everything we can to bring Lucy home safely. We have officers involved at the moment in enquiries, but anything you can tell us, anything at all, could help our search."

Any further attempts to question her proved hopeless. The detectives left Brenda in the capable hands of Molly Kelly her housekeeper, who had been with the family since Brenda herself was a baby.

Interviewing Molly established similar facts: Lucy was to stay with Abigail. Molly had helped her pack and told officers which clothes were in her overnight bag. Neither that bag nor her school backpack, nor indeed her cello had been found. Through red-rimmed eyes, Molly related the events leading to Lucy's last sighting.

"Nora, that's my daughter, was to collect Lucy from school and drive her to Abigail's house after calling in at the optician to collect my glasses. Poor Nora had toothache for several days. She's so scared of dentists she put off doing anything about it. It got so bad that Brenda came across her in the kitchen crying in pain and insisted she attend to it immediately. 'I'll arrange the appointment myself,' she told me and asked George, that's Nora's boyfriend and the family's repairman, to collect Lucy."

The detectives learned that changes in arrangements happened regularly and would not have been problematic for Lucy. George was now out of town attending a computer course. Nora did not expect him back for a few more days or even longer than that.

The last contact with him was a call from the airport saying he had missed his flight and was booked on a later one. Nora giggled like a school kid when explaining that no, she hadn't heard from him during conference week.

"I accepted his reason for me not to contact him as I'd only be a distraction. He said he would call again when leaving for home. He never liked to be disturbed."

Later that day, Detective Carr entered the highly scented premises that were advertised in bold lettering above the door as Gina's Floral Boutique. She found the scent overpowering, drew a sharp intake of breath and approached the owner, who immediately left a floral display she was working on to attend to her.

"You're here about Lucy, aren't you? I haven't slept a wink since she went missing. My daughter is distraught and I can't think straight. Have you news?"

Gina locked the door, turned the notice to "Sorry. Closed" and led the officer to a sitting room at the rear of the shop. She reiterated what they already knew.

"Lucy was to be dropped off here by a staff member. As far as I was aware, they were calling at the ophthalmic optician before coming here to eat pizza and take in a movie, then return here for a sleepover. Not that much sleep ever takes place on these occasions; the girls normally chat and laugh well into the night. I was to take her home after lunch in time for her music lesson. That was the usual arrangement I had with her mom."

"When did you find out Lucy wouldn't be coming to stay?"

"Abigail came home from school quite disappointed at the change of plans. She told me Lucy had sent a text to say she was sick and would take a rain check. Abigail tried to call back but had problems connecting."

Gina could shed no more light on the situation.

Back at headquarters, Detective Carr joined her colleagues to consider statements gathered to date and stated, "We have still to interview Abigail when she feels more composed, and George North when he returns from his conference. So far, we have drawn a blank in the investigation."

Another officer gave his report. "The school principal recalls seeing Lucy go in the family sedan and drive off with George at the wheel. She regularly saw him pick Lucy up. Sometimes Nora, the house maid did the school run and occasionally Brenda herself. School personnel knew the household staff well. There were no issues with Lucy. She appears to be a model student, regular kid, hard-working, popular with her peers. Seemingly, she had a unique musical talent and her ambition was to travel the world with a top orchestra. She had already performed in public with the school band. As far as the principal was concerned, having spoken with staff, the kid had no problems that anyone knew about."

"How can a kid simply vanish?" mused Harvey. "We have loads of loose ends to tie up before I put more officers on the case. Where is the sedan? Has it been returned to Brenda's house? We need to examine it, and quickly."

"Why has there been no ransom demand? This mother is mega rich," Detective Carr asked no one in particular. "I would have expected a demand by now."

A forensic team arrived to examine the sedan. Molly showed them to the garages where the family cars were stored. Only then did they discover that the car used to transport Lucy from school was not in its usual place.

"Didn't anyone notice that car was missing?" an incredulous officer asked Molly.

"I seldom come to this part of the estate. I garage my car in a different area, near my apartment. Only Nora and George would have any cause to come here when they are driving for Brenda or Lucy."

"We have to contact George to shed light on this," continued the officer.

When questioned, Nora told officers the venue for George's last conference, as far as she could recall, and presumed he would be there again.

"He attended several of these courses. I don't remember where they all were, but I can list one or two."

A colleague of Harvey's assigned to locate George North's current conference reported that no such I.T. meeting had taken place at the stated venue for some time.

"We stopped holding conferences here more than a year ago," stated a caretaker. "The building was sold on and is used now for different purposes."

Further investigation established that George North had indeed booked a flight but failed to show.

***

Some days later, a car-parking attendant reported a Cadillac Deville on the third floor of a multi-storey car park, approximately fifteen minutes from Lucy Mears' school. A team of officers sent to examine the vehicle found Lucy's school backpack. They did not locate her cello or mobile phone. Fingerprints lifted from the car were compared to those held on record by members of the Mears household following an attempted burglary some months previous. These prints had been necessary for elimination purposes. There were no prints other than those of current members of the household. Where was

George North? Priority was given to tracing him and hopefully locating the missing girl.

The distressed mother was kept informed at every stage of the investigation. She remained at home, too upset to attend to her business empire, which she said was in the capable hands of her trusted team with whom she was in regular contact. She was reluctant to leave should she miss a call on her home phone. Molly continued through tears to run the household, albeit with much less enthusiasm. Nora, distraught at the news of George's non-existent conference, could shed no more light on his whereabouts.

"This is so unlike him, Mom. What has happened to him and Lucy? They could be lying injured somewhere."

"Honey, the hospitals have been checked and they haven't been taken there. It's all so confusing!"

CHAPTER 3

On the shores of a lake, many miles from the scene of the mysterious disappearance of Lucy Mears, the weather had abated slightly. The campervan had come to a halt, allowing the occupants a few days' respite from further travelling and an opportunity to assess their situation.

"Perhaps we ought to cut back on the sedation," suggested the man, "to one drop a day. The kid has never been fully alert, she poses no problem and we do not want to overdose."

They decided in future to administer only one evening dose. As if on cue, the girl rallied and through slurred speech struggled to implore once again, "Call Mama."

For several more days, the trio continued to live by the lakeside, secure in the knowledge that poor weather and their secluded position would afford them total privacy. With the reduction in sedation, Lucy Mears slowly emerged from her trance-like state to the realization of her plight with two people she had never seen before.

***

Both detectives Harvey and Carr interviewed Ken Farmer. He was a refined man in his late sixties, a confirmed bachelor, he informed his enquirers, married to his music. He had been giving Lucy Mears cello lessons from an early age, having been alerted to her talent by her school music teacher, a fellow member of the local orchestra. He was upset to hear of Lucy's disappearance and could not offer any insight as to where she might be.

"I came to the house, as usual, only to be told she wasn't available for her lesson."

The distraught man became silent for a moment, as if deep in thought, then continued.

"I found that strange, as I was always informed in advance of any change of plans."

At the time Lucy vanished, he had been in his local library where he had spent a good part of the afternoon researching his passion: the history and restoration of musical instruments.

The librarian, a rather stern woman, looked aghast at the mere thought of someone questioning the sweet man. She was a tall, extremely thin person. She wore her grey hair in a middle parting, pulled back off her face and tied in a bun that was held in place with a butterfly clasp. Her half-moon glasses perched on her sharp nose gave her a look of superiority, which no one would dare question.

"He sat over there at his usual table in the corner, where he read in total privacy. I made sure no one disturbed him. He comes here regularly; you can set your watch by him."

Detective Carr suspected that perhaps she was secretly in love!

Later, Lucy's friend Abigail felt able to answer some questions and, in the presence of her mother, told of the last time she saw her best friend.

"It was break and we were having lunch. We talked and planned for the sleepover. Lucy was so excited to be coming to mine. She loved being with Mom and me. We were going to eat pizza, see a movie and Mom was to pick us up after that to bring us back here for a sleepover." Abigail continued with her account. "Lucy was in music class after lunch. I was at my art class, so I didn't see her again. I expected to see her in the locker room at the end of the school day, but when she wasn't there I thought her class had finished early and she had gone off with her ride."

Detective Carr paused from asking questions to allow the upset girl to compose herself.

"Take your time, Abigail, you're doing really well. Carry on when you feel ready."

"Lucy was to be picked up as usual by car. She was never allowed to walk home, unlike Abigail who normally walked the short distance," volunteered Gina.

Abigail continued. "I was surprised to get Lucy's text saying she was sick and taking a rain check. I tried to call back, but a message said the number was unobtainable. It was very strange. Her phone had been working earlier in the day."

Detective Carr left Gina's Floral Boutique and returned to HQ to follow up what she had learned. The appointment at the optician had been cancelled, the message purporting to come from a male member of the Mears household. This led Carr to enquire about the other supposed appointment, that of Nora's emergency dental visit. Nora had indeed visited the dentist, the appointment having been arranged by Brenda Mears who had requested George collect Lucy from school.

"Nora had been miserable for days," said Brenda. "I made the appointment myself."

She assured the detective that it was not unusual for her to arrange such things.

"I look after my staff," she retorted sharply.

***

Weather at the lakeside had eased enough for the trio to take short strolls to stretch their legs, giving Lucy her first whiff of fresh air. Too weak to walk unaided, she was escorted along on the arms of her minders, dragging her feet and stumbling as she went, mumbling incoherently. The only recognizable sound appeared to be her plaintive cry of '"Call Mama". For several more days, they continued these walks, which always finished with mild sedation for Lucy on return to her warm detention. Rested and revitalized, the minders decided to set off on the next stage of their journey, crossing into yet another state.

**

Detective Harvey called the team together for a brainstorming session, which resulted in more questions than answers.

"Why has a ransom demand not been made?"

"Did the kid go off with a boyfriend?"

"Did she meet someone on the internet perhaps?"

"Where is George North?"

"What happened after that car was left in the car park?"

It was time to call in the media. They already had a whiff of a missing kid but as yet had few details.

"The kid's mother is reluctant to go public, but we have to overrule that."

Harvey called a press conference and related as much as he felt necessary. A quick result from the TV appeal brought a member of the public to the door of 1st District Central, where Harvey worked, to report a sighting of a Cadillac as it entered the car park.

"I thought it strange for a posh car to be in that rundown car park. I was exiting the place and had to break sharply or I'd have been in a head-on when it raced towards me. I didn't give any more thought to it until I saw the appeal on TV for information."

When questioned further, the witness recalled seeing a speeding green or blue car leave the place shortly afterwards. Officers were instructed to locate the car ASAP, if for nothing more than to eliminate it from enquiries.

A few crank calls from overly unhelpful members of the public delayed the important work of the team. Eventually, a woman called to say she had reported such a car to her local police. It had been parked in a manner making it difficult for her to manoeuvre her car from her driveway. The car appeared abandoned from about the time of Lucy Mears' disappearance. Forensics pulled some prints from it. They belonged to Lucy Mears and an unknown person. The car was found near an alley leading to a dilapidated bus station in Halsted.

Brenda was more hopeful that her daughter would be found on hearing that some progress had been made from the media appeal. She still waited for a ransom demand to be made. Lucy's computer showed no worrying internet activity, as she expected, stating Lucy's passion was her cello.

"I could not imagine Lucy being interested in internet activities like social networking sites. She allowed nothing to distract from her music."

Enquiries were made to bus companies about the evening the child vanished. Very few vehicles were at the bus depot around the time in question. One driver did not continue his journey beyond there, as his vehicle developed a serious fault requiring towing for repair. Another driver remembered the ferocious night in question, but did not recall a child among his passengers.

"Few people ventured out that night, sir," he stated. "It was a foul night!"

One driver, however, clearly remembered a weeping girl on his coach accompanied by a middle-aged man. He presumed her misery to be associated with the coldness of the bus. They exited at Wentworth, the final destination.

"I didn't see where they went. Everyone had heads down trying to shelter from the weather. The bus had been so cold; folk just wanted to get home."

An appeal went out to trace passengers from that bus, not an easy task, as the depot was a hub-centre, taking people on other routes and to other states.

Some days later a call came through to Harvey. A passenger had come forward confirming the presence of a young girl travelling with a man. The witness had been sitting across from them.

"I was concerned about her. She moaned constantly. I presumed like the rest of us that she was cold. The guy with her didn't seem to communicate or comfort the poor kid. I myself fell asleep and only woke up when we reached Wentworth. They were ahead of me for a time, walking towards the east side of town to Lox Road where I lost sight of them when I turned for home."

"No one seemed to be out and about that evening, sir," reported officers assigned to find the location described by the passenger.

An appeal went out; door-to-door enquiries were made around Lox Road and surrounding streets. The residents were asked to recall the night in question and report anything unusual in the area. The police had a breakthrough when a householder told of a delivery van that cruised her street. She watched as it slipped and skidded on the icy road as the driver attempted to read the house numbers.

"It came to a halt at number 28A Lox. Not that I was being nosey!" she exclaimed. "I was looking out at the weather when I spotted the truck; it was slipping all over the place. We never get our streets treated for ice, you know; something should be done about it."

A warrant was issued to search the premises of number 28A. A team of officers entered the building in the early hours of the morning, taking the householder by surprise. The place was dusted for fingerprints and sent for checking. The occupant, a woman in her fifties, appeared bemused and agitated at the activity in her home. She claimed to have no knowledge of a truck at her door and had no idea, she said, as to why her house should be searched. Attempts to trace the truck proved futile; major companies had no record of their vehicles being in the area on the night in question and smaller companies too gave similar responses.

CHAPTER 4

Brenda Mears had never experienced anything other than luxurious living. Both her parents had come from wealthy families and had accumulated fortunes of their own, before meeting at a business convention.

Brenda's mother had died giving birth to her. Her devastated father threw himself into his business ventures, rearing his infant daughter with help from his sister-in-law, Anna. As if to atone for his child's deprivation of a mother's love, Simon Mears spared no expense in the raising of his daughter. Her aunt privately blamed the child for the death of her only sibling and unfortunately, on occasion, was unable to refrain from being outspoken. This led to tension in the already stressed household, to the extent that Anna felt unable to continue looking after her niece. She intimated her intention to return home to her antique business when suitable help could be found for the hapless father and motherless child.

Molly Kelly, recently widowed and with a young child of her own to care for, was grateful to find such employment and entered the life of the Mears family. The sister-in-law, relieved of her task, returned to her own home to come back on only one occasion: to attend Simon's funeral some twenty-five years later.

Brenda's early life was predictable for an only child reared by a rich, doting father. She wanted for nothing. Simon talked to her about business matters from an early age as if she were an adult on equal footing, fostering in her an interest and knowledge of the firm that she was destined to inherit.

This would stand her in good stead later in life. After completing a post-grad degree in business management, she joined her father in the firm and progressed rapidly to a position on the board of Mears Empire where, through time, she would become its chief executive. She enjoyed life to the full, dated several students during her college days, but her first real love was for a high-flying politician. She thought her future was with him, but on hearing of her unplanned pregnancy, he swiftly abandoned her, saying marriage and children were to feature much later in his plans.

A devastated Brenda gave birth to a daughter whom she called Lucy.

Lucy Mears came into a world of opulence. The devoted love of Molly, her main minder, and that of her besotted grandfather made up in some way for any apparent lack of interest shown by her mother. Simon Mears, now terminally ill, lived long enough only to see his beautiful granddaughter take her first faltering steps. Molly's daughter, Nora, helped her mother rear Lucy and became a close, almost elder sister to the child. Molly never forgot that Lucy belonged to someone else. It saddened her to witness the apparent absence of Brenda in the life of the child.

Brenda's inheritance from her father and the legacy held in trust from her mother's estate, coupled with her own prolific appetite for work, ensured she continued to live a lavish lifestyle. As her business ventures expanded over the years, she amassed not only a considerable fortune, but also a formidable trusted team of associates, devoted to their employer and her ideals.

Bob Lees, young, enthusiastic and talented, joined the team in the early years of the growing business under Brenda's regime and soon became a valuable group member, becoming romantically involved with Justin Palmer, the other gay person in Brenda's elite company. The two set up home together and became engrossed in each other and in their work, adding valuable input to the business.

Olivia and Ron Scott, a married couple, added energy, vision and clear-thinking to the firm. They were currently on holiday, cruising on their private yacht in the Caribbean. The holiday ended abruptly when Ron's elderly mother suffered a stroke. Brenda granted unlimited leave to allow them to organize care for the elderly woman, whom she had met on several occasions and was particularly fond of.

The eldest associate, Myra Hill, was a formidable woman, a financial whiz who had been headhunted by Brenda. Myra kept abreast of the company's financial status, advising, cajoling where necessary, and convincing the board of the best available investments. She was promoted to the position of chief financial officer.

During Lucy's absence, the company continued to function normally, with Ron and Olivia offering to return home if required. Brenda insisted that they remained where they were to arrange care for the frail parent and assured them that the other team members were in agreement with this decision, adding that they were a tower of strength to her. They would be recalled if necessary and were thanked for their concern.

Armed with background information about the Mears Empire, Harvey and Carr interviewed the board members in turn. On the afternoon of Lucy's disappearance, Bob

Lees and Justin Palmer were in their respective offices, working until seven in the evening, when they left to dine at their favourite bistro. A cleaner remembered seeing them leave the building.

Myra was out of the office most of the day having meetings with the firm's accountants, returning about five-thirty to collect some files to work on at home. She spoke briefly to Justin before heading for home. This alibi checked out.

Next day they were all in their respective offices when Brenda ran screaming from her suite, having been told by Molly of Lucy's disappearance. They were understandably shocked and upset. Myra drove the hysterical woman home and stayed with her and the distraught Molly for some time. She arranged for Brenda's car to be delivered to her home. Justin and Bob wept copiously for the rest of the day. Via Skype, they contacted the Scotts to give them the devastating news.

**

The travelling trio, having refuelled and stocked up with grocery provisions, had now crossed three states. The adults, concerned that Lucy was overdosed, cut back yet again on the amount of sedation. The girl while still drowsy became more aware of her surroundings. She seldom spoke except to mumble a mantra, Call Mama. The rhythm of the engine and gentle music lulled her to sleep which lessened her awareness of the tedious miles of travel that had been imposed on her.

CHAPTER 5

Fingerprint results from house number 28A clearly showed those of Lucy Mears, as well as the householder, Clara Blake. Officers returned to the house to take the occupant into police custody, where, under pressure and scared out of her wits, she confessed to harbouring the girl for four days. Through a deluge of tears and interspersed with sips of water, the woman constantly dabbed her eyes and confessed her part in the disappearance of Lucy Mears.

She had been in debt for several years without seeing a way out of her problems. She had taken a loan from a dubious source and got behind with instalments. She feared for her life and that of her family due to some menacing-looking people sent to demand ever-increasing payments from her. After a stressful few months she was approached with a solution: take in and look after a kid for a few days until given further instructions and the debt would be cancelled. She had no idea who delivered or collected the girl but gave a rough description of the man. She was upset at having had to administer sedative and had kept the vial, which she handed over to police. This was sent for analysis and was to prove a valuable clue. Clara Blake ignored instructions to incinerate the kid's clothes. Never having seen such quality in clothes she had them laundered and passed to her granddaughter who was delighted to own such designer outfits.

Clara Blake was held in custody for her own safety

pending further investigation into her involvement in the ever worrying mystery of the girl's disappearance. Fearful for the lives of her family, Clara was unable or unwilling to give a useful description of any of the thugs who appeared at her home demanding money, but she did assist a photo-fit officer in providing a reasonable likeness of the man who delivered the girl into her custody. This was shown to the bus driver and the one passenger who sat near her. They both agreed that with slight alteration, the picture could be that of the man on bus fifty-three. It was circulated to the media.

It was not George North.

Officers retrieved paperwork from Clara's home to begin intensive investigation into tracing the loan sharks.

Attempts to trace George North drew blanks. Media appeals were increased across all states. Nora became increasingly concerned about her boyfriend, adding to the already high stress level in the Mears household. She had first met George when he applied for and was accepted for the post of live-in caretaker and repairperson some four years earlier. Soon, they began dating and became an item. Nora claimed he did not reveal much about his past.

"I sensed there was some tragedy in his early life. I didn't push for information. I thought the guy would tell me in his own time. In his spare time and off-duty days, he attended I.T. classes, seemed knowledgeable about computing and program-making. It wasn't unusual for him to accumulate time off to attend conferences. He was obsessed with computers and had a store of I.T. magazines."

Officer Carr prodded. "Was he jealous of Brenda Mears' wealth, do you think?"

"Not so much jealous, probably just a bit envious, but

he appreciated that Brenda's success came from hard work, and it gave him a hunger to improve his life. He was generously rewarded for his work here, as we all were, but he wanted more."

A search of his rooms produced nothing of interest. No background papers, letters, photographs or anything that would shed much light on George North. His computer was impounded and sent for analysis.

Nora, more from anger than anything else, was determined to solve the problem of George's non-existent computer conference.

"How could he lie to me?"

She checked out websites for recent I.T. courses but found too many to probe. She narrowed her search to within one-hour flying time and contacted venues, establishing that no one of that name had registered with them. She widened her search and located a college where George North had registered for a seminar around the dates in question but had failed to attend.

No airline company would release passenger information to her, but Detective Harvey, following up her research, found details of a flight booked by George on the evening of Lucy's apparent abduction. Officers were sent to the airline to investigate.

Young Wilson Blythe, a police I.T. expert, called Harvey to report some interesting findings on George's computer. Along with Detective Carr, they huddled round the screen while Wilson explained his findings.

"Right then, what do you have for us, Wilson? You know I'm a dinosaur when it comes to computer stuff!"

"This is a list of flights booked by him over the past ten months, several day trips, presumably on his days off. There were also longer trips like the recent one he was meant to be on but cancelled. He often seemed to change his mind about flights. Maybe to throw people off his trail, do you think, sir? The trips were booked in his name and he seemed to have travelled alone."

"You have a point there, but why? Why would he want to avoid detection if his trips were legit? How could he afford to pay for these trips? This guy has some answers to give us if we can ever locate him. He sure as hell knows what happened to that kid."

CHAPTER 6

George North had always been ambitious. Born into a poor family, he watched his parents struggle to hold down several jobs to provide for their young family of which George was the eldest. A quiet couple, they taught their children right from wrong, to be respectful, honest and hard-working, which rubbed off on their son and his siblings. As a teenager, he had a weekend job with a delivery firm and visited parts of the city he had never seen before. He was in awe of the rich and aimed to improve his lot in life. He studied hard, discovered a talent for computing and basic programming and was determined to establish his own business.

Just as he was planning his future, his father died in a work accident. His future was now uncertain and his college dream crashing before it had time to take off. His mother's health failed and his young siblings were relying on him as the breadwinner. He moved from job to job, always aiming for a better life and never swaying from his ambition. After the early demise of his mother, his two young sisters moved to Wisconsin to be cared for by relatives, while he drifted from place to place, working at whatever he could until he saved enough to purchase his first computer and hone his skills with help from occasional I.T. courses. He applied for yet another change of employment with better prospects; a position that he assured himself would be a temporary move.

He found himself employed and living in the Mears household. He soon became an integral, trusted part of the establishment. His friendship with Nora developed into love with the blessing of Molly who was glad to think of the prospect of her daughter settling down with a good husband.

The couple talked of marriage and children. This served only to fuel his ambition and his hunger for what he saw as a better life for them both. In spite of the generous salary from his employer, his need to update his I.T. equipment drained his finances to the point that he had to search for a loan. Unknown to him, his troubles were only beginning.

Lucy, slightly less sedated, emerged from a fog, her mind darting between fuzzy memories to semi-reality. "George... where are you? where am I? My cello... Call Mama... so cold, air blowing on me, my legs... cold, cold... snow... George... man in green car... cold bus... warm now... so sleepy."

Her new home lumbered on through changing scenery, stopping for regular rest periods for the sake of the child. The area allocated to her for a bedroom was cosy and tastefully furnished. It gave her some privacy.

***

Detective Harvey contacted Ron Scott by Skype and conducted an interview from which he ascertained his and Olivia's whereabouts during their absence from Mears. They had indeed flown from Chicago O'Hare to Bridgetown, Barbados, and sailed from there. Proof of this was recorded on their logbook and confirmed by marine officials. Ron's mother's illness was genuine. Hospital authorities confirmed that Mattie Scott was a patient of theirs and was visited daily by her son and his wife.

Olivia Scott, overcome with emotion over young Lucy, took her turn on Skype and confirmed her own whereabouts over the past few weeks. Weeping tears of exhaustion, she implored the detective to find little Lucy, such a sweet child.

"We are coming right home," she said. "We will be of more use back home than sitting here worrying about everything. In any case, our holiday is over."

Brenda, persuaded by Molly to get out of the house, returned to work, albeit for only a few hours a day. She spent time less working, rather consoling the emotional Justin and Bob. Myra, always the strong one, rallied around encouraging everyone to focus on the work tasks in hand, while privately sobbing at Brenda's plight, wishing fervently that someone would demand a ransom or, God forbid, Lucy would be found somehow or other.

Fatigued from travel, Ron and Olivia Scott arrived back at the headquarters of Mears Empire. They gathered in Brenda's office suite with the others, consoled, wept and hugged like the close family they had become over the years and bound together now by a common cause. Brenda briefed them on events since the fateful day of Lucy's abduction and updated them on the latest police report.

"I have every confidence in Detective Harvey and his team from C.P.D. They are working flat out to find Lucy. I don't understand why no one has demanded a ransom. God knows I can afford it."

Ron and Olivia had begun their holiday two days before Lucy vanished. This concerned Detective Harvey. *A coincidence, or what*? he thought to himself. *Worth investigating further*. He discussed his concerns with his deputy.

"What's your take on this, Carole? Am I being paranoid about those two?"

Detective Carr knew well how her boss's mind worked. He left no stone unturned in his search for the truth and if he felt that something was amiss, it was worth investigating.

"It is a bit odd that they were absent from Chicago at the time of Lucy's disappearance. I can see where you are going with this, Tony. You think perhaps they have colluded with a person or persons unknown – George North perhaps, since they would know him from their dealings with Brenda. Go with your instincts and have a background check done on them. I'll set it up if you like, if only to eliminate them and get us on track."

Intensive checks were made on Ronald Scott and Olivia Scott and showed nothing questionable. The timing of their holiday was a mere coincidence.

***

The campervan developed engine problems in Wisconsin. Lucy and her female minder settled once more in a motel while the van was taken for repair. The abductor, tired of the tedious journey, welcomed the opportunity to allow her young charge to rest up. The girl became quite distressed now that her sedation had been decreased, allowing her to think more clearly.

"Please Call Mama. What is happening to me? Who are you? Where are you taking me?"

"Hush, child," comforted the woman. "No one will harm you, you are safe, and soon you will be home."

Lucy did not recognize the accent, thinking it to be that of a foreigner. Worn out, she sobbed into her pillow and slept soundly.

Many miles away, a call was made to a secure line.

"Speak," was the curt command.

"Good evening, Boss, reporting in."

***

Mears Empire continued to function as normally as the staff could manage. Each executive member out of loyalty to Brenda attempted to banish, at least temporarily, thoughts of Lucy's plight and work on their various remits. Sobbing could be heard from time to time from their various offices.

Detectives Harvey and Carr arrived unannounced at the premises with a warrant to search all offices of the board members, assuring Brenda it was a routine part of their investigation and that they would leave no stone unturned in the search for her daughter. Computer equipment was removed to be examined for anything untoward. Officers asked to examine the yacht belonging to the couple, only to discover it had been sold before the couple left the Caribbean to fly home. Instructions were given to locate, search and if necessary impound the yacht.

CHAPTER 7

Brenda's team of close associates was each interviewed again. Bob Lees joined the Mears group as an enthusiastic participant, always giving one hundred percent to his work, never faltering in his devotion to his employer who had head-hunted him having heard of his skills. He was given more responsibilities than he could ever have imagined. He became chief operations officer in charge of shipping publications for Mears, not only to every state, but far beyond. He purchased his first home, a luxury apartment in an upmarket part of town. Just when he thought life could not get much better, Brenda employed Justin Palmer and, within a few months, they had become an item and lived together in Bob's apartment. On hearing of Lucy's disappearance, Bob stated that he was at work that particular afternoon, engaged in shipping details.

"I met Lucy on several occasions," he told the officers, "and had the joy of hearing her play her cello at home when Brenda had one of her many dinner parties for the team. She was a great believer in team building. Lucy had such talent, such a sweet child. We were invited to her music room where there was a little stage for private performances from Lucy. We spent an idyllic hour listening to her play, firstly, on her beautiful baby grand piano, then on her cello."

Tears welled up in Bob's eyes and, before he could give

vent to his emotions, the officer thanked him for his time and took his leave of the upset man.

Justin Palmer joined Mears Empire after spotting an advert for a graphic designer and seeing off other contenders for the post. He settled quickly into the lively and hectic life of the company. His joy held no bounds when he found a soul mate in his colleague Bob. He, too, had met young Lucy at her home and was distraught at her plight.

"Whenever I look at that poor mother, I want to dissolve in tears. I have to keep strong and support the firm by carrying on as normal, but things are anything but normal now. Lucy has such a musical ability, sir, amazing in one so young. Please God that she is found safe and well and that there is a reasonable explanation for her absence."

His alibi checked out, as did Bob Lees. They were eliminated for the moment from the enquiry.

Detective Harvey still had misgivings about Ron Scott and his wife despite intensive enquiries throwing up nothing of concern. The couple seemed genuine and squeaky clean. Harvey could never dismiss a coincidence and the subsequent selling of their yacht, which was somewhere in the Caribbean under new ownership, bothered him greatly. He interviewed them separately.

Olivia Scott joined Mears shortly after Justin. Her main remit as a director was to liaise with customers, obtain contracts and ensure that Mears honoured them quickly and professionally. She knew that she and her husband were fortunate in working for such an inspirational boss. They each had different skills, which they utilized to the full to ensure Mears Empire went from strength to strength.

Having recently secured a lucrative contract, Brenda,

delighted with their success, had granted extended holiday time to allow the couple to indulge in their passion for sailing.

"We flew to Barbados, picked up our yacht, *Stella-Night* which had been moored there since our last holiday." Olivia continued. "Ron's brother, Sam, who lives in Bridgetown had use of it too. We stayed with him and his family for a few days before we set sail. Not long into our trip, we heard Ron's mother had taken ill with a suspected stroke. We returned to port and took a flight to be with her."

It was during that time that Myra Hill had contacted them with the devastating news of Lucy's abduction.

"Ron spoke to Brenda," said Olivia, "offering to return home immediately, but Brenda insisted we stay and attend to his mom."

"When did you sell the yacht?" probed Harvey.

"Not long after that. We had a family conference," she continued, "and decided the cash would be needed to fund the old lady's long-term care, as it was obvious that she would never live an independent life again. Ron dealt with that."

Harvey thanked Olivia and proceeded to interview Ron Scott. He confirmed in detail the account given by his wife. He swore allegiance to Mears Empire and was eternally grateful to his employer for her understanding during his mother's illness, especially in the horrendous circumstances in which Brenda found herself struggling on a daily basis.

"We were distraught to hear about Lucy, but Brenda insisted we stayed where we were, promising to keep in touch via Myra's Skype. About the sale of *Stella-Night*, we felt it was the right time to sell; we were so immersed in work that we had little opportunity to sail." Ron paused, as if mourning the loss of his beloved yacht. "My brother used it on occasion but not often enough to warrant continuing ownership. We wanted to secure a future for our mother who needed to be in an assisted care home. So we decided to sell up. *Stella-Night* is now under new ownership."

Ron produced a bill of sale, which his brother had faxed, giving details of the new owners.

Harbour authorities co-operated with Detective Harvey's team. They located *Stella-Night* and escorted it to port for inspection. The new owners, a local couple, stunned to be involved in any questionable dealings regarding the yacht, were in dread of losing their recent purchase, but accepted reassurances that they were not under suspicion and agreed to allow a search of the vessel.

They were interviewed in depth in order to satisfy officers of their non-involvement and were quickly removed from enquiries. Their fingerprints were taken for elimination purposes. After several days the boat was returned to them when officers had completed their examination, lifting several prints to be investigated further.

Sam Scott, Ron's older brother, was questioned about the sale of the yacht. He was partially disabled and used a walking stick to aid his mobility.

"As you can see, officers, I am not a fit man. I had an accident some years ago that left me with walking difficulties. I don't get around too well. Occasionally, I would sail *Stella-Night* around the bay, more to keep her ticking over than anything else." His eyes lit up as he described the yacht. "She was a beauty! A forty-eight-foot motor yacht, a Skipper liner motor yacht. Ron loved that boat, but with his high-powered job, he seldom had opportunity to sail her. When our mother got sick he made the brave decision to sell *Stella-Night* to help pay for her long-term care. He gave me a generous allowance to help fund my trips to visit her. Couldn't find a better brother, officers, if you searched the world! Neighbours of ours who loved sailing jumped at the opportunity to purchase her. The sale of *Stella-Night* went through without any hitch."

Harvey was unsure of Myra Hill.

"She's too cool, too calm. She knows more than she lets on. Bring her in for more questioning."

Myra Hill had had an interesting career. A high flyer since college days, she sailed through courses and landed lucrative work in the financial industry, and moved up and onwards through several firms. She had a great capacity for lifting failing companies out of difficulties. She came to the attention of Brenda Mears who recruited her not because Mears Empire was in any financial danger, but to secure its already high standing in the business world.

Focusing on her career, Myra's marriage failed. She was ready for a change of direction when Brenda Mears secured her for her firm. Brenda had her checked out, contacted previous companies she had worked for and gave her a six-month trial period, at the end of which Myra Hill was rewarded with a permanent position.

Bucking the trend during a recession, Mears Empire increased its productivity, amassed yet more millions in profits and elevated Myra Hill to the inner circle of Brenda's trusted team. Despite probing, Detective Harvey could not fault Myra Hill's honesty and concluded that the woman had a hard shell around her, seldom allowing people to crack it open and get to know the real Myra.

CHAPTER 8

The travellers set off again, crossing state after state, covering more ground by night to ensure Lucy slept naturally without sedation. In daytime hours she watched movies, dozed, ate, played some board games with her captors and, weather permitting, took gentle strolls in places well away from public view. Mile after mile, the scenery changed, becoming dreary at times, spectacular at others and always subject to the weather.

Lucy's minders remained calm, reassuring and helping her to be less stressed now that the decision had been made to stop sedation. A calmness and peace descended the little home and had it not been for the situation all three found themselves in and the atrocious weather, it could have been a haven of tranquillity. In a strange way, Lucy felt safe with them, safe, but bewildered.

Lucy's attempt to communicate with her captors proved difficult; her companions were pleasant, looked after her as well as they could, but spoke in a language unknown to her. The only word she could make out was, "Zelda", the name she presumed was of her female traveller.. Feeling brave, the girl called out,

"Zelda, please Call Mama!

Hearing the girl use her name, Zelda looked stunned, glowered at her partner for letting her name slip and launched in to a tirade of abuse aimed at the unfortunate man. She soon calmed down and attempted to reassure the frightened girl that all would be well and soon they would reach their destination where everything would be made clear to her.

"Soon, child, soon!"

As the investigation continued, media appeals had some success.

A sharp-eyed shopper remembered seeing a man resembling the guy driving the green car in her local grocery store.

"I noticed him because of his dishevelled appearance and his foul odour. I presumed he lived rough."

The store owner also recalled the man and later told officers, "He became a bit of a regular customer. He only ever bought beer and from the look of him I don't think he ever ate anything. He was no problem, sir, always polite and well spoken."

Officers searched the area around the grocery store and in a nearby wooded area well away from passing traffic located a small tent. Unaware of his impending arrest, a man slept soundly.

Dale Greer was taken to the local police precinct and interviewed for some time before coming clean about his involvement in the Lucy Mears mystery. Like Clara Blake, he too was the victim of loan sharks. He was unable to repay his loan and was "invited" to follow specific instructions: to collect a girl from an associate, drive her to a nominated bus depot and travel with her to transfer her to an address that would be given to him when he picked up the girl. He was to administer a sedative in a drink before boarding the bus. Released pending further investigations, he was asked to stick around.

"I hated having to do that, sir," he sobbed as he told

officers. He stood up to leave the precinct. "I have kids of my own and would be out of my mind with worry if one of them went missing. My family were in danger and I had to agree to take that kid to New York."

Carr questioned her boss's decision to release the man from custody.

"Tony, sir, we can't release him, he is essential to this enquiry. He could go off radar."

"Trust me on this. I want him followed. I think he might lead us to young Lucy, and at the end of the day that's our main concern."

Dale Greer returned to his makeshift home, unaware that officers observed him from a distance and that his every move was being monitored.

Detective Harvey reviewed case notes to date and pondered over them before calling another brainstorming session.

"Is there a report on the attempted break-in at Brenda Mears' home?"

"Yes," replied a young officer. "I filed the report myself; there was not much in it. No entry was made to the house and the owner was happy with our quick response and let it rest there."

"Pull the file… now!"

Harvey could be brusque.

The officer set off and returned with a flimsy, short report, which he proffered to Detective Harvey to read and pass to Carr.

"Not much there to go on. An opportunist perhaps?"

On the evening of the attempted break-in, George North was alone in the house working on his computer.

Molly and Nora were having an overnight stay with a

friend after a visit to the theatre. Lucy was at Abigail's home engrossed in a school project and Brenda was at her office, not expected home until late in the evening. George, busy with his programming, was alerted to sounds outside on the gravel path. He turned to the security camera to see two figures snaking towards the house. He turned off the security camera, darted downstairs, opened the door to the duo and stepped outside to receive an envelope.

The men departed into the night, leaving no trace of their presence. George called Brenda Mears to report that intruders had been caught on camera but scampered when the lights came on.

"No need for alarm," he assured his employer.

Brenda was already preparing to leave the office and asked George to call the police to check out the area as a precaution. Reassured that no attempt had been made to gain entry to the house, the police left after a cursory glance at the security camera.

"Seems like you disturbed them, sir. I don't think they will be back, opportunists for sure."

"Was the security camera ever checked out?" asked Carr. "There's no mention here about it having been examined."

"Check it out as soon as," hollered Harvey to the flummoxed young officer. "Get that tape from the house now!"

Harvey and Carr, bringing with them every minute piece of evidence, every thought, idea and suggestion accrued during their investigation, summoned all officers involved in the search for Lucy.

A lengthy resume took place with each person presenting his or her findings. They offered explanations in more detail when anything was unclear to any of the squad. Detective Carr charted each item of information on a large flow chart.

"This is no normal kidnapping: no ransom has been demanded, no threatening calls. What are we missing?" Harvey continued to muse over the chart. "We must dig deeper. George North is involved in some way. We have to find this guy, and soon." He thumped his desk in frustration. "Re-interview everyone! Get to it!"

"If we can eliminate some of these names and narrow it down, we can get at the others in more depth," concluded Carr.

Extra officers had been drafted in to speed up the ever increasingly frustrating enquiry. The squad worked long hours, determined to bring an end to the issue. Cases involving children touched the hearts of many police officers. Those with children of their own were determined to bring Lucy's abduction to a swift conclusion and the perpetrators to justice.

Detective Carr couldn't remember when she last had a full night's sleep. At home, she hugged her two kids as if scared to let them out of her sight.

"I love you guys!"

CHAPTER 9

Harvey turned his attention to the Mears' house. Brenda agreed to her house being searched. She was at her wits' end, desperate for news of her only child.

"Why, oh why has there been no ransom demand?" she sobbed. "I have money enough to pay. Should I offer a reward, Detective?"

At times Brenda thought progress was too slow. She liked to be in control of events and the lengthy enquiry frustrated her as it did Harvey's squad.

Harvey thought that offering a reward would only bring time-wasters, cranks, people who would swear to have seen Lucy go off in a spacecraft and such like.

"Best leave that for the moment, until we investigate further. I have to ask, how was your relationship with your daughter? Were there any issues we need to look at?"

Brenda took a deep breath before answering.

"We had the usual mother/daughter spats at times, nothing serious, you understand. Lucy is at that age of wanting to exercise her own independence, make her own decisions, I suppose like any girl of her age. We did have some words recently about her future career, but nothing that would be problematic, Detective."

"Could you expand on that?"

"There's not much to say really. Lucy wanted to study music as a career. I approve of her music as a hobby, something to pass the time, but as a career? No! I expect her to follow the family tradition."

Deep in thought, Brenda was silent for a moment before continuing.

"My father and grandfather, and indeed my great-grandfather, built the business from nothing to what it is now, a highly respected, profitable concern. Lucy is young, she will see that tradition has to be maintained. It's not a major issue." Brenda dabbed her eyes. "I planned to discuss it with her, get her to put things into perspective and come around to my reasonable way of thinking."

"Could she have seen it differently? Enough maybe to make her run off? I'm clutching at straws here, Brenda. We have to explore every possibility, however painful."

"Lucy would never do that. Where would she go?"

"Perhaps with help from someone... a friend maybe? Could Abigail have colluded in this... is that possible?"

"I don't know what to think now. My mind is in turmoil."

Detective Carr, who had been silent during the conversation, suggested, "What about George North, Brenda? Would Lucy have gone with him? Was she close to him? You know what teenage girls are like, they can be infatuated by older men, especially as Lucy doesn't have a male parent. Could she see George as a substitute role model?"

Brenda was horrified at this suggestion. "How dare you say such things! Sure, George and Lucy are close, as are all my staff; they are comfortable with each other. Lucy would never go off with him; the very idea makes me sick."

Detective Harvey, attempting to defuse the situation, said, "Neither of us wants to upset you, but, as I said, we have to look at every possible scenario here, no stone left unturned, so to speak. The priority is to find your daughter and return her home to you. However distressing it may appear to you, we are only doing our job."

Silently, he thought the answer lay with Brenda Mears herself. He wondered if she could have, for whatever reason, arranged the abduction of her child. The very idea made him shudder. Detective Carr noticed how ill and gaunt Brenda had become.

"We'll return later with some officers to have a look around the premises here, just routine, but it has to be done."

Driving back to headquarters the two debated the latest thinking.

"Let's check out Abigail again... perhaps the kid is hiding something. Kids of her age have strange ideas and often confide in their best buddies."

Harvey laughed. "You talking from experience, then, of your own wild days?"

"I admit, I was a bit of a rebel. I did the opposite of what my parents wanted. Mind you, if Lucy is as talented a musician as we are led to believe, it seems criminal to force her to give it all up to join the family business, however successful it is."

"But is it enough to make her run off? Could George North have aided her and where on earth are they? You touched a nerve when you mentioned that to Brenda. Hell, is it possible that she and North have gone off together? That hadn't entered my mind. I've been thinking more along the lines of him having abducted her."

Later that day, both detectives talked to young Abigail, with her mother present.

"Abigail, we want to find Lucy soon to keep her from danger. Do you know anything about her disappearance at all? Please level with us here, this is getting serious."

Abigail was taken aback at the line of questioning and looked to her mother for reassurance.

"Sweetie, just tell the detectives anything you know. Sometimes even the smallest remark can mean something."

"Mom," sobbed Abigail. "I miss Lucy, I want her found too, but I know nothing, absolutely nothing!"

Detective Carr probed gently. "What about boyfriends, Abigail? Was there anyone special in Lucy's life, did she have a steady boyfriend?"

"Certainly not! Lucy was too focused on schoolwork, especially her music. Sure, she had friends among the boys, we both did, but that's what they were, just buddies. I think the guys in her music group were a bit in awe of her."

"So, she had no special guy then, no one she dated?"

Abigail laughed at the mere suggestion of her friend dating anyone.

"Not Lucy. We would chat about boys, about who we liked and disliked… all the kids did, but, no, Lucy had no time for anything other than music."

"Did she ever talk about how she got on with her mom?"

"Yeah, she would offload. It was no secret that her mother was strict. Lucy only really chilled out when she came here. Her mom wanted her to go to business school and follow her into the family firm, but Lucy was adamant she wouldn't go down that road… yeah, it caused tension."

"Enough, do you think, for her to run away?"

"You don't mean that! Lucy would never run off. She would have confided in me if such an idea crossed her mind… which it didn't. That's a crazy thing to say."

"Thanks, Abigail, for your input… just one more thing,

do you think she could have gone off with George North, or could he have helped her run off?"

"George? Nora's guy? No way would she be with him! It was great fun to be around him and Nora, they were an item, very much so. Lucy and me, we thought he was really old, at least thirty-five."

They both smothered a laugh at that.

CHAPTER 10

A team arrived to search Brenda's house. Attention focused firstly on Lucy's suite of rooms. Her bedroom to a certain extent was typical of most teenagers. Posters of celebrities adorned the walls, in between an array of pictures of composers and musicians. Similarities with most other kids' rooms ended there. Next to her bedroom was a dressing room filled with designer clothes, shoes, bags. No expense had been spared in the rearing of Lucy Mears. Her computer was taken for checking; it showed mostly schoolwork, assignments, musical scores and information connected with her performing arts studies.

The music room where she had her cello lessons with Ken Farmer would make any music student green with envy. A small stage was set at the far end, with a few comfortable armchairs arranged as if a performance were a regular event. An empty cello stand was a poignant reminder of the ongoing saga of the missing child. A beautiful baby grand took pride of place in the room.

Staff quarters were examined and revealed nothing sinister. Detective Carr was impressed by the standard of accommodation afforded to Brenda Mears' employees.

Molly had her own comfortable apartment that she had shared with Nora until her daughter moved into a similar, but smaller apartment with George North, an arrangement that Molly frowned on for some time, until she accepted how happy and contented her daughter had become. She was fond of George and looked forward to having him as a son-in-law.

Molly told them how she herself had been in a happy marriage with Charlie Kelly, a farmer well known in his community as a decent, hard-working guy. They were enthralled with their baby daughter, Nora.

"I wanted my daughter to have a secure, happy life with George, like I had, until…"

Molly hesitated as if recalling memories that pained her.

"Life was good," she continued, "but tragically when Nora was only three years of age, her father was killed in a horrendous farm accident. Too gruesome to go into, Detective. We had to leave there as the rented farmhouse belonged to the farm owner who needed it for his next work tenant. Callous though it seems, that was the way of things. It was for the best as I couldn't have faced looking out towards that field where…"

Molly was fortunate to obtain a position of live-in housekeeper, being recommended by her friend Sally who had been cook to Simon Mears for as long as she could remember. Sally wanted to retire to live with her niece in Florida. Molly had never expected it would be easy to find live-in accommodation with a young child in tow and was overjoyed to be employed by Simon Mears.

He explained that he required a full-time helper for his baby daughter and was grateful to have Molly take over the rearing of his child to allow him to concentrate on his business ventures.

Molly bonded with baby Brenda and raised her with her own daughter, conscious always that the child belonged to her employer. Molly's daughter, Nora, was a constant playmate for the young Brenda. They became loyal friends, shared everything and thrived on Molly's love.

The girls took different paths after finishing high school. Nora took up a college place, studying hotel and catering management.

Molly continued. "Nora had a dream of owning and running her own small hotel. We were grateful that she was in employment alongside me."

Brenda, on the other hand, attended university and obtained degrees in psychology and business management. She took up a position within her father's firm and soon became an equal partner. Brenda enjoyed life to the full, working and playing hard. She dated several men and fell hopelessly in love with an aspiring politician.

"He swept her off her feet," continued Molly. "She wouldn't listen to me when I said I had bad vibes about the guy. Call it the Irish in me if you like, but I usually read people well. I did not warm to the guy." Molly took a deep breath before continuing. "Her future seemed secure, until she became pregnant. The furious politician told her marriage and children were not part of his immediate plans. He cruelly abandoned her. She sat here at the kitchen table with her father, Nora and me. We were all three concerned and distressed at her plight. She swore us to secrecy about the name of the baby's father. Brenda was adamant. She told us, 'No one must ever know who he is. I will tell my child when I think the time is right, but now, I do not want to hear his name mentioned ever again.'"

A few months later, young Lucy Mears was born and entered the lives of Molly and Nora.

Nora answered Detective Carr's questions honestly and openly. She was still in shock at discovering her George was not the man she thought he was.

"I feel I don't know him at all," she moped. "We fell in love shortly after he came to work for Brenda. I was attracted to his quick wit, his hard work ethic and ambition. He was a joy to be around."

"Was he resentful of Brenda Mears' wealth?"

"Not so much that as envious. He was determined to branch out in his own business when he had enough to set himself up in the computer world. He supported my dream of someday owning a hotel. I had no idea where he went on his conferences and I.T. courses. I never asked. I trusted him. I took his word for it that he was at a computer course. Where is he, Detective? He is innocent of these whispered accusations. He and Lucy could be injured somewhere, lying in a ditch or something. He loved her like the rest of us and she trusted him implicitly; he could never harm her."

"Was there any change in his behaviour recently, can you recall?"

"Come to think of it, yes! Some months ago he came back from one of his conferences, bright-eyed and happier than I'd seen him in a while." Nora smiled as she recalled happier times. "He had purchased a new, state-of-the-art Mac and was ecstatic when it was delivered. Over the next few months, he lavished gifts on me, jewellery, flowers, and meals. 'You sure we can afford this George?' I asked. 'Honey, don't you worry your pretty head about this, everything's under control, babe,' he said to me. I'd never seen him so happy."

Detective Carr asked as gently as she could, "Nora, I have to ask you a sensitive question, please don't be upset, but we have to probe every minute piece of information and ideas in order to bring Lucy home. Is it possible that George and Lucy have run off?"

"WHAT!" screamed Nora. "No, not my George. How could anyone think such foul thoughts about my George? We all adored Lucy, but as for anything else, you are way too wrong!"

"Nora, sometimes in my job, I have to ask very disturbing questions. It's best to have things out in the open."

Nora sobbed uncontrollably. Detective Carr left her in the care of her equally distressed mother. Both women were still traumatized at the turn of events in what had been a previously peaceful existence.

"Detective," said Molly as she led them off the premises. "Will we ever see Lucy again?"

Carr patted her on the back and whispered, "I hope so. I really hope so!"

CHAPTER 11

Lucy became more agitated with each passing day, forcing her minders to reinstate a mild sedation.

"I dislike doing this," said the woman, with concern in her voice.

They trundled on, across ever changing landscapes, stopping every now and again for respite. Their preferred resting place being secluded motels where they were out of sight of public areas.

"This must end soon," exclaimed Zelda to her partner. "The child has been through enough. This weather is brutal."

The couple had decided since Lucy now knew the name of her female captor to use it freely. Zelda's partner introduced himself as Kristof but would not give any other details to the inquisitive girl.

"We have to follow instructions, too much is at stake, Zelda We must continue to travel this road until recalled by Boss." He sighed in resignation. "It won't be long now. I have to call tomorrow for further instructions."

The campervan was more than satisfactory and of the highest quality available. No expense had been spared to ensure their journey would be as comfortable as possible. The trio were becoming increasingly weary and the two captors concerned at the strain placed on their young charge. They longed for it to be over.

***

Harvey's squad assembled once more to tackle the increasingly worrying abduction of the fifteen-year-old girl.

"Come on, guys, we have to come up with something! The kid's mother is a multi-millionaire. Anyone looking for money would have demanded a ransom by now."

"Seems to me, sir, it's an inside job. Probably an employee of Brenda Mears," said a young officer, keen to be seen to be involved in the biggest mystery to hit Cook County in as many years.

"Where is George North? Who is he really?" asked another officer in frustration.

Using the whiteboard, the team recapped: a list of all those involved in any way were listed, names crossed out when they were eliminated and the team sure of their innocence. Question marks remained beside those who were still suspects. Number one suspect: George North. Number two suspect: Dale Greer.

***

Ken Farmer dined alone in a smart diner where he was a regular customer. He dined on wholesome food accompanied by one glass of good wine. As he ate, a sealed envelope was placed on his table.

"I was asked to give you this," said a waiter.

Ken Farmer read the contents of the envelope, put it safely in his pocket, smiled, paid for his meal and left the premises. Returning home, he made a call to be told, "The consignment is on its way."

***

Brenda Mears increased her time at the office, throwing herself into her latest project with a fearsomeness that frightened her staff. When reality set in, she wept copiously. Myra, always alert to the needs of her boss, put a comforting arm round her shoulders and silently wept for the increasingly futile attempt to find Lucy. At home, as sleep evaded her, Brenda's despair grew deeper, her pain increased. An ominous silence descended on the household.

Molly continued with her chores, pride no longer in her work. Her heart was heavy with anguish. Nora, bereft for Lucy, confused about George, became more lethargic with each passing day. It was a dismal existence.

***

"Sir," called a young officer to his superior. "Can you come to the computer room? I think I've found something interesting!"

Harvey listened carefully as the young expert explained his findings.

"I re-checked those CCTV tapes of the intruders at Brenda Mears' home some months ago. Something regarding the tape rankled so I worked on it and came up with this... look here, sir... someone has tried to erase part of the tape, very amateur attempt, if I might say so."

"Get on with it. What have you found?"

Harvey could be brusque and short tempered when under pressure. The case in hand caused him sleepless nights and he often took his bad temper out on anyone nearby. Those who knew him avoided the raging storm by remaining professional during the onslaughts, knowing that calm would prevail.

"There appears to be three people at the door. This is fuzzy, but you can just see the outline of the guy inside the door. He seems to be accepting an envelope or some kind of small package. If I'm not mistaken, it's George North."

Harvey looked closely at the screen. "But he told us the intruders ran off when he put the outside light on. There's no outside light in this film. It's essential we find this guy. George North is up to his eyes in this mess. I'll put out an A.P.B. on him. Can you identify the other guys?"

"Too dull, sir, but what I can deduce is approximate height. I'll keep working at it, but I don't hold out for much improvement."

"Good work, Simpson!"

"It's Timpson, sir," said the young man as Harvey left to report these findings to his task team. Calm had returned. Officers were allocated witnesses to re-interview.

Abigail, Lucy's friend, was once more interviewed alongside her mother, Gina. Both were still distraught. Abigail, a tall child, had her mother's striking blue eyes and sharp facial features that drew people towards her magnificent smile, which unfortunately had been vacant for some time. Her blonde, curly hair swept in waves across red-rimmed eyes. She constantly pushed her tresses from her eyes, but the uncontrollable locks defied her attempt at any kind of order.

"I wish I had contacted Brenda when Lucy called off her sleepover," sobbed Gina. "I was so busy supplying flowers for a wedding to even think of calling to find out if the sick kid had recovered."

Abigail had tried to text, but Lucy's mobile number was registered as being no longer available.

"I thought it kind of strange, but didn't follow it up. I was so disappointed that Lucy had called a rain check. I helped Mom with the wedding flowers and thought no more about it, thinking she might contact me when she felt better."

Ken Farmer was unable to be interviewed at the precinct. Officers called at his apartment, a neat two-bedded place, tastefully furnished to suit his bachelor lifestyle.

The décor and furniture were exquisite. No expense had been spared by the somewhat eccentric gent. He wore a tailor-made three-piece suit and cream shirt that was adorned by a red bow tie. His long grey hair had a hint of silver through it, giving a salt and pepper effect. For all the world he gave the impression of being an absentminded professor.

"Thank you for coming here, officers," he said. "I am waiting for an important delivery. I collect and restore old musical instruments. I'm expecting a unique cello today, courtesy of a friend of Mario, owner of the local bistro that I frequent. Mario left a note for me to call to confirm delivery. Today's the day!"

"Quite a collection you have here, sir," commented one officer casting an untrained eye over the pieces that almost filled the workroom. "We would like to ask you some questions about Lucy."

Ken confirmed he had known her since she was eight or nine years of age.

"I was introduced to her by the school's music teacher who told me of her amazing talent. The child had a quarter-size cello, which she played like a professional. Her mother was keen for her to have regular lessons and I was honoured to be invited to enter the life of such a gifted young musician. Her school had a fine music section in the performing arts programme, where students spend two years on music theory and become involved in orchestras through all levels from beginning to symphony. Lucy has played at school concerts on many occasions, such a rare talent!"

Ken could shed no light on the girl's disappearance and was visibly overcome when talking about her. Satisfied that he had no involvement in the mystery, the officers began to leave when a truck arrived at the musician's home. An elated Ken took possession of the long awaited cargo and went into raptures as he opened his treasured package.

"This beauty," he explained to the officers, "is a unique Pietro Floriani cello, made in Germany around 1875. Cellos were invented in Italy, you know. That is where most of them come from, but to get hold of this German model fills me with so much emotion. These cracks you see here," he said, pointing them out to his guests, "cause buzzing. Each piece of wood vibrates differently. This is spruce; the spruce top is the sounding board. I hope to restore it to its former glory. I so wish to show this exquisite instrument to young Lucy."

He sighed with a mixture of joy, elation and sadness.

"We will take our leave of you, Mr. Farmer. Thanks for your time. Enjoy your cello."

Harvey and Carr spoke to Lucy's classmates, who were stunned and upset at her disappearance.

"She sat with me in music class," commented one student. "When I couldn't get the piece right she helped me fix things. She had a cool way about her, could explain things so I could understand. We are all really worried about her. She's a really cool kid."

"Yeah, wish we could help find her," a spotty-faced, serious-looking kid added. "We sure miss her from class. Lucy's a brill musician."

Evelyn Cosimini, a delicate, dainty creature with dark brown eyes and flyaway hair, was Lucy's music tutor. She told of her last sighting.

"We were packing up, ready for home. The kids were chatting about their plans for the weekend ahead. Lucy mentioned she was having a sleepover with her friend Abigail." Wiping a tear from her eye, Evelyn continued. "'I'm so excited,' she told me. 'I love being with Abbie and her mom, Gina. Gina's a fun mom!' Gina arranged the flowers for my sister's wedding. We chatted about that and the bridal outfit, as females do, and off she went, quite happy and well. I was puzzled to hear she had called off her sleepover as she was sick; that was before I heard about her abduction. It's so worrying, Officer. Poor Ken, her home music tutor, is distraught, as are we all."

Satisfied that no further light could be shed on Lucy's disappearance from teacher or students, the officers returned to base.

"That confirms it then, the kid was not sick, so it seems likely her abductor put the text through to Abigail and discarded the phone."

Investigators had tracked down George North's sisters. Jessica Crawford was living in Wisconsin and had lost touch with her brother since childhood and knew nothing of his whereabouts. She had married in her early twenties, moved away, reared her children and seldom thought about him and the family's early existence. She kept in touch with her sister, Mary-Lou, who had moved to Ohio after marriage.

"I doubt if she would have anything to add, Officer. She was the youngest and has little memory of George or our parents."

Jessica recalled a little of their early life. Her memories

were scant, recalling it as being a happy, but poor home, until tragedy struck with the loss of her parents.

"Our mother couldn't cope after Dad's death. I remember her just sitting in the old rocking chair, weeping as she hugged us, telling us to be brave. George seemed to be the one who cooked and cleaned and looked after us."

She wiped a tear from her eye, memories of those early days long suppressed, but now foremost in her troubled mind.

"George," she recalled, "was a kind brother. When it was decided we should move to Wisconsin to live with an aunt, he explained, as best he could, what was to happen to us, despite his own loss. Mary-Lou, I remember, was excited at the prospect of a long road trip, sleeping in George's arms for most of the journey. We were met in Wisconsin by an aunt and uncle, our mother's aunt and uncle really, farming folk who made us welcome and gave us a good life with them. We thrived on good, wholesome food and love. Our relatives were elderly, but often said our coming to live with them gave a new lease of life and put a spring in their step. George stayed for a few days then returned to Chicago to take up a college course.

"We exchanged cards and letters for some time, but these soon became less frequent and eventually dried up as we all got on with our lives. I hope George will soon be found. He ain't in no trouble, is he?"

Jessica Crawford had obviously not heard about the missing child of a million dollar business woman from Chicago. She was parochial in her interest of what went on in the world and to her, Chicago would seem a million miles away. Not wishing to upset the innocent woman, officers assured her they were just making routine enquiries about an ongoing case. They wished to spare her unnecessary distress.

"If her brother is involved in something sinister, she will hear about it through time. At the moment, ignorance is bliss," commented an officer as they left to report to Harvey.

Ensuring no stone was left unturned, officers visited Mary-Lou Cooke. She could not add anything to the investigation, knew nothing of her brother's life, barely remembered him and only recalled hearing of him from her sister. She was tiny in comparison to her sister. That they were kin was evident from the almost identical facial expressions, colouring and demeanour.

"I kind of remember a long bus ride, but nothing else of my early life other than being with my relatives on the farm in Wisconsin. Jessica would tell me stories of our life in Chicago with our parents. Sadly, all I have to remember them by is a faded wedding picture. I called my first son George, for my brother."

Mary-Lou produced a faded sepia picture showing a sombre couple posing outside a church building. Both sisters resembled their petite mother. From the most recent picture of George North given to them by Nora, he bore a striking likeness to his father.

"Should he happen to turn up here, ma'am, please get in touch."

Enquiries from George North's sisters did not add anything more in the investigation and mystery of Lucy Mears.

CHAPTER 12

"Has anyone asked about former employees of Mears Empire?" asked Carr.

"Get to it, find out names and locations of all former employees going back as far as necessary, and find out if anyone had a grudge against the company or the owner."

Myra Hill unearthed lists of former employees, from the time before Brenda took over from her father. Teams of officers worked on finding those people: some had died, some moved from the area, no trace being found for several of them, but investigations continued. Brenda was asked if anyone stood out in her mind of former employees who perhaps held a grudge. Molly, who was in the room, remembered something.

"What about that creepy English guy with the funny name? I never liked him, came around the house too often for my liking. Ellis something…"

"I know who you mean." Brenda scowled.

"Barclay Ellis-Jones. He was employed by my late father. He was very attentive to me when Father passed away."

"Too blooming' attentive, if you ask me," muttered Molly. "Never away from the house, any old excuse."

"What happened to him then?" asked Harvey.

"I had to dismiss him. He had been siphoning off money for several years, only small amounts at a time, which went unnoticed until one of the auditors discovered something wrong and had him investigated. He had been helping himself for years. Ended up in prison."

"He's worth investigating," commented Harvey as he turned to leave.

"But that was so long ago, Detective. Lucy was only a tot. He hardly knew her."

"We have to check every small detail. He probably has nothing to do with this, but we have to investigate. If we can eliminate him we can concentrate on others," concluded Harvey.

Several days elapsed before news came through of Barclay Ellis-Jones. He had indeed been imprisoned for embezzlement, not just from Mears but also from a few other firms he had wheedled his way into.

"Served his time in prison, then went off the radar," commented the investigating officer who had done the research. "I've put in a call to a guy I know who works for CID in London. He will ask around and get back to me if he can find some background on the dude."

"Good work, man," complimented Harvey.

Barclay Ellis-Jones was born in Poplar, East London, and changed his moniker from plain Barry Jones to a more affluent-sounding one, double-barrelled for effect, worked on ridding himself of his accent and set off to seek fame and fortune in America. Arriving there, he applied himself by any means available to the task of ingratiating himself into a life more suitable to his dream. He charmed his way into several companies and moved from one job to another, astutely storing up information from each.

He became employed in a thriving publication firm in Chicago whose fortunes he had followed for some time. He began working for Mears Empire and soon rose through the ranks from one department to another; his sharp mind and quick learning ability saw him progress rapidly and come to the attention of the then owner, Simon Mears, Brenda's father.

Simon Mears had taken over the business from his late father.

At that time it was only a small publishing and distribution set-up, catering for local needs in the community. Simon had a vision to expand into education publication. Cook County Education Department gave him his first major breakthrough: a contract to supply textbooks and printed material for colleges and schools throughout the county.

Chicago ranks only second to New York in the publication industry. Simon Mears determined to be one of the best, and employed people whom he could trust in the building of his dream and insisted on top quality products and service. Mears' fame became synonymous with professional standards, fair costing and excellent customer service. His business expanded, necessitating a move to better premises in a more prominent part of the city.

Mears' reputation spread throughout the area, giving employment to several hundred people. Conditions for staff were excellent; the owner ensured only the best was available for his ever increasing army of workers. Daily, he would walk from department to department to get to know his workforce and enquired from some about their family. He had a genuine interest in his people and would often arrange for small gifts to be sent to anyone who was sick.

He was on the lookout for a top quality financier, interviewed many, discarded most and finally employed a young, well-spoken, enthusiastic Englishman, Barclay

Ellis-Jones, whose credentials, on paper at least, were impressive.

Thanks in some way to Barclay Ellis-Jones' input, the firm expanded rapidly. Unaware of a devious side to the man's character and trusting the guy implicitly, Simon left much of the financial responsibility to Mr. Ellis-Jones. He was unaware of any financial irregularities in his firm. Widowed at a very early age, Simon sought solace in his empire building, his work being second only to caring for his daughter who enjoyed listening to her father's account of his day's work, his employees and his plans. Illness struck him down in his prime.

After her father's death, Brenda Mears took control of the firm. She was familiar with each department and the general running of the business, having been a junior partner since obtaining her university degrees. She understood the intricate nature of Mears Empire, its ethos, its community involvement and its financial matters. Initially she accepted at face value Barclay Ellis-Jones' support after Simon's demise. Over the ensuing months, he often appeared uninvited at the house with many enquiries, several of which could have waited until the next day. He became irritating. He wrongly sensed Brenda's demeanour as loneliness and attempted to ingratiate himself into her affections.

"You should get out more," he suggested. "Why don't you and I go out to dinner, take in a movie and relax a bit?"

"No thanks, Barclay, I've too much to do, let's take a rain check."

The rain check never materialized, but the incorrigible guy continued with several such requests.

"You and me, Brenda, we could be quite a team."

He leant forward and whispered in her ear, much to the disgust of his employer.

"Get off me! Let me be! I'm not going out with you; you're not my type…"

Failing miserably, he became embittered when she dismissed his advances and planned to revenge this rejection of him. "Someday, lady, you will be sorry you ever crossed me," he murmured to himself.

CHAPTER 13

Rogue moneylenders operated a lucrative business, targeting vulnerable people who usually hung around bars, spilling not only their drinks but also hard luck tales to anyone within earshot. Overheard by loan shark crooks, they were often rescued from their plight with promises of instant dollars, never more than a few thousand at a time to entice them to sign up. Too inebriated to think clearly, they signed paperwork completely oblivious of interest rates, fees or penalties for late payments. Such illegal activity had interest rates rising in some cases to three hundred percent, too steep for victims to repay. Often fraudsters resorted to enforced payment by blackmail or threats of violence. Within this criminal fraternity, the corrupt Barclay Ellis-Jones found a niche. His smooth-talking, charming manner made it easy for him to build up a profitable business in a vile trade. To his unfortunate victims, he appeared as a charming financial saviour.

Dale Greer had been an innocent victim of banking mismanagement, which had led to the global crisis in the banking industry. He lost his life savings and his house was foreclosed, his wife and sons left to the care of relatives, while he tried to pick up the pieces of his shattered life. He developed a need to escape through alcohol. He spent most of his time and money in seedy bars attempting to escape his miserable existence. His drunken rant in a bar was overheard by a fellow drinker, a well-dressed man who listened to his blustering conversation about the injustice of it all. His new buddy encouraged him to continue with his sorry tale, while plying him with more drink.

Clara Black had lived most of her life in a rundown area of New York. Her marriage failed, leaving her to raise her son and daughter by herself. She held down two jobs, took in sewing but never seemed to manage her household bills. She resorted to petty thieving, mainly from grocery stores in order to feed her family. Her teenage son got into trouble with the law and was jailed for drug dealing, burdening his mother with lawyer's fees that she had no means of paying. After yet another court appearance and watching her wayward son jailed for a second time, she took refuge in a seedy bar near the courthouse and, having over-indulged, poured out her troubles to a stranger who encouraged her to drink and talk.

On one of his legitimate visits to New York for a computer study weekend conference, George North became increasingly frustrated with his own financial situation, not helped in the least when one of the instructors commented that his computer was way out of date and if he wanted to attend further conferences, he would have to purchase a more up-to-date machine. This for George spelt disaster. He would either have to abandon his plans to set up in business or somehow or other get his hands on some cash. He joined some others from his conference for a drink at the bar and when they left to have dinner, he stayed for a few more drinks before heading off to wander the streets to clear his head.

He found himself outside a bar in a none too salubrious part of the city and was enticed in by the smell of alcohol and the sound of raucous laughter. His drunken rant was overheard by a fellow drinker, a well-dressed man who listened to his rambling conversation about the injustice of life and encouraged him to continue with his sorry tale, plying him with more drink.

To Barclay Ellis-Jones' team of rogue money lenders, further evil criminals found a niche. Alfred Wysoki was a violent, gun-carrying criminal who had spent time in Cook County correction boot camp, re-offending some years later, resulting in a mandatory three-year prison sentence. It was there he befriended Barclay Ellis-Jones, imprisoned for four years for embezzlement. Barclay Ellis-Jones had already served most of his first year sentence when Alf, as he called himself, shared his cell and his life. A third cellmate was Les Soubry. The three compared criminal history, outdoing one another with their tales of bravado. They contrived a get rich quick scheme for their release and made the decision to move east to the Big Apple, which suited Alf who wanted a fresh, albeit corrupt start. Alf was proud of his criminal past. He had several facial scars and with his broken nose and staring eyes fronted an air of foul, menacing superiority, confident that no one would mess with him.

"There ain't nothing mechanical I can't mess with and crack; safes are a walkover, and as for autos or engines of any kind I can fix or fiddle whatever's required. I'm ace!" boasted the crook.

Freed from incarceration, Barclay Ellis-Jones dropped his middle name, calling himself Barclay Jones and saw himself as *Mr. Barclay Jones, Money Lender of Repute*. He was an expert at changing his accent, becoming a polite, well-spoken Englishman or a southern gent, changing from his west coast accent to east coast and on occasion resorting to his native east London cockney accent, all of which made witness identification of him a difficult task.

He travelled to New York and rented a small basic apartment in the Bronx.

Alf joined him some time later and the pair began their illicit money-lending business and searched for vulnerable or needy customers, mainly from poorer areas of the city where poverty was rife, people wide open to tempting loan offers from the suave, polite-talking Englishman offering sympathy and ready cash to free them from their misery. Later, Les, released from prison and living nearby, joined in their shady business. Barclay Jones, having hidden thousands of dollars from previous crimes, funded the illegal scheme.

"I'll recoup my money in no time at all," he told Alf as he laid the ground rules. "Maximum of $2,000, easy repayments, what they can afford, starting $5 or $10 weekly, to get them hooked. We draw up paperwork, they will be so out of it when they sign, they won't know the rate of interest we charge. Give them a few months' respite before calling round for repayments. I don't want you turning up with the cash at the bars. How about we use crazy Les to do the donkey work?"

"He ain't so crazy. I had many conversations with him in the prison library. He's a qualified pilot and an engineer. A really clever dude. Got into trouble drinking on duty, did drugs, got himself dismissed and jailed. Used to fly all types of planes, from big commercial to private ones. Told me he once flew some VIPs to the White House."

"Good, we'll make use of him. Right, Alf, you're in charge of collecting repayments in cash. Turn up at their house and one look at your ugly mug, they will pay on the nail."

"Or pay the consequences. Wow, I am gonna love that bit, buddy," sneered Alf.

"Not too rough at first Alf. Take it gently, show them your sweet side, and then, when they can't pay, go in for the kill."

"Yeah, man, the charges will escalate through the roof. Bring it on!"

CHAPTER 14

The 19th January 1996 was the day Amila Tanovic's life changed forever. She was exhausted from non-stop nursing, attending to emergencies pouring in to the hospital where she worked. The task was relentless; medical supplies were in short supply, staff morale at a low ebb and space at a premium as more and more casualties piled in, the strain etched on each face.

The war in Bosnia had taken a toll on its people. Unrelenting violence against inhabitants of her home city of Sarajevo reduced them to a state of constant fear. Nowhere was safe in Sarajevo, not work, school, home, nor hospital. Deliberate attacks on the hospital had already reduced a section of the building to rubble. The death toll rose daily as the siege of Sarajevo continued relentlessly. It was the longest siege of a capital city in the history of modern warfare.

More and more victims were being brought in by any means possible, by family, friends, and compassionate strangers. Constant demands rapidly depleted the already limited supplies of bandages, drugs and basic equipment. Amila, in early stages of pregnancy, worked on autopilot. Blood stains covered her uniform, face and arms. There was no time to clean up, no reason for a change of uniform – finding a fresh one was now out of the question. The noise of heavy machine-gun fire constantly filled the air, assaulting eardrums and spreading panic and dread throughout the city. An explosion was heard nearby, causing alarm in the hospital.

Word came quickly: a tram had been attacked not far from where they were and soon more casualties were carried in. Amila looked up momentarily from attending to a young man whose arm had been severed to see her distressed husband, Nikol, carrying a wounded victim, tension etched on his handsome face as he frantically looked for a space to place the casualty, his police uniform unrecognizable now from weeks of the ravages of war.

"Amila, dragi, darling, such tragedy. A tram was attacked, a grenade was fired from Grbavica neighbourhood. Such carnage. One person dead, many injured, about nineteen, we think. When will it end?"

Amila helped her husband place the injured man gently in a corner space, hugged Nikol and wished, how she wished, she could stay there in his arms and rest her exhausted body.

"I have to get back, honey, so much to do, so much… I will come for you later to take you home. You must rest soon. Think of our little one."

He tenderly kissed his wife and took off once more into the carnage of the city.

Home, a name that should conjure up images of peace, tranquillity and safety, was none of these. Their little haven had been reduced almost to rubble in an artillery attack that took the lives of Amila's parents, grandmother and young sister. They lost most of their personal possessions, documents, birth and marriage certificates, family photographs and treasured mementoes.

Nikol's family had been wiped out in a previous air strike, his brother still missing, whereabouts unknown. The couple, along with Sergei, Amila's only brother, escaped because fate decreed they were not in the vicinity at the time. The three shared what was left of the family home, one room barely big enough for them to move, but it was luxury compared to what some other people had. Tragedy again struck when Sergei was shot by a sniper's bullet while out searching for food.

While tending to casualties of the tram attack, Amila collapsed from exhaustion. Doctor Josef, attending nearby, rushed to her aid, noticed the flow of blood on the floor and feared the worst.

"Another innocent victim," he sighed.

Several hours later a worn out Nikol arrived to be told the devastating news that Amila had lost the baby they so longed for.

"Take her home, Nikol, let her rest, find nourishment from somewhere and get out of the city as soon as Amila is strong enough to travel. It will be a difficult journey for you both. Thousands of our fellow citizens have already left. May your God go with you!"

"What about you, Doctor? Will you leave?"

"No, Nikol, I have work to do here. I am needed to care for my injured fellow citizens. My wife and family are safe in Germany with her cousin. I will remain here in the city I love, until I am forced to leave. I weep for my Sarajevo, such a picturesque, cosmopolitan city."

Doctor Josef bowed his head, composed himself and continued.

"All three ethnic groups lived harmoniously. We worked and lived together in peace until propaganda sowed seeds of doubt in the minds of frightened people. I must remain, but you, Nikol, you must get out soon. You are young and your future is elsewhere. Go to America, the land of the free, build a new life there. I have not yet told Amila that she will no longer be able to bear children. I must go to her now."

For almost a month, Nikol tended his young wife. Amila's grief for their loss was carved on her face, the horrors of past atrocities haunting her every waking moment, her every dream. In sleep, she called out for her family. Nikol cursed the war and resolved to leave as soon as Amila was strong enough to travel. With the city completely blockaded, life was harsh, electricity cut off, water was in short supply and communications became difficult.

"Get well, my dragi, we will leave this accursed place and go to America, the land of the free, where we will begin our new life with hope in our hearts."

Amila, spurred on by the promise of deliverance from the hell of their existence, took the meagre nourishment offered to her and began to emerge like a fragile butterfly from its cocoon, shaking off her dark mood and setting herself to help sift through their few belongings and pack what was practical to carry.

When Amila was well enough the couple joined thousands of other Sarajevos making their escape from their war-torn city. They queued for long periods to board a bus with other frightened refugees. People who would normally behave courteously now pushed and shoved, elbowing their way to find space for themselves and their pitiful belongings. Nikol guided his still frail wife to a seat, settled her as best he could, and faced a long, dangerous journey to freedom, conscious always of the threat of attack at any time. Amila slept for most of the journey, while Nikol, always alert, kept watch from the barred window for signs of danger. Many hours later, the driver refused to go any further. His passengers walked in convoy, huddled closely together, as if human contact would protect them from onslaught of attack. They hitched rides by any means. A farmer piled as many terrified people as he could onto his cart, took them a few more miles before having to leave them to their fates.

"Halva, thank you," shouted the crowd to their helper as he drove off to attend to his own pitiful life.

Various means of transport eventually conveyed them to the outskirts of Zagreb where, dishevelled and exhausted, they took refuge in a disused railway carriage and sheltered as best they could from the cool of the evening. There they attempted to rest, always anxious, always alert and never totally relaxing.

The couple were approached by a man who offered to obtain documents and passports for them at a hefty price, promising them flights to freedom. In desperation, Nikol handed over a good part of his savings and waited. Days passed. Just as they feared they had lost their savings, the man appeared with paperwork that he assured them would pass scrutiny at any port or border. He took them and other refugees to a safe house where they waited several more days for his return. Amila rested well, with the anxiety sitting on the shoulders of her young husband. At length the man returned, escorted them to the airport and handed them flight tickets to Germany.

"Sorry, my friends, not enough money for your choice of America. It's the best I can do in these hard times. Good luck to you. I wish I could do more, but these are dangerous times."

With that, he vanished into the night. Such was the chaos at the airport that harassed officials herded passengers to waiting planes with only a cursory glance at documents.

"Hurry along, people, keep moving."

Much to the relief of the couple, the plane taxied down the runway and took off, leaving them to adjust to new identities. Nikol studied the new forged passports and smiled.

"Goodbye Nikol and Amila; welcome Kristof and Zelda," whispered the new Kristof to his smiling wife. For the first time in days, the newly named Kristof slept.

CHAPTER 15

The new Kristof awoke with a start when the plane touched down in Munich. With other refugees, they were taken to camps where they spent many weeks. Germany had agreed to take a limited number of Bosnians and had almost reached that limit. Kristof, fearful that they could be deported at any time, wanted to leave the camp as soon as possible. He had limited funds hidden in his possessions and with the help of another couple whom they had befriended, left the camp and managed to purchase an old, well-used car that they prayed would last long enough to take them to safety. The four of them headed out of Germany, aiming to reach England.

"That's the plan, Amila— sorry, Zelda," he corrected quickly. "If the vehicle lasts that long!"

Their companions, an older couple, Marc and Donata Stojanovic, dreamt of a new life in New York with relatives and were pleased to befriend Kristof and Zelda and share their travel plans. They shared the driving and nursed the old car along, grateful to cross Europe. Donata, a motherly woman, took Zelda under her wing, giving the fragile younger woman a sense of security she had long forgotten. Donata was a jovial, rotund woman, well used to hard work. Her weathered face was etched with pain as she spoke of their losses during the mayhem of war. As the four travellers shared experiences of living through war, they wept, laughed and planned their futures with hope in their hearts with each passing mile.

Marc, a hard-working farmer whose leathered skin was browned by years of working outdoors, showed such strain that he appeared much older than his seventy-two years. His energy, however, was intense. When they were forced to leave their home he attempted to take a goat with them on the bus. Donata laughed at the memory of it, as she shared the story.

"Marc was pushing the goat onto the bus, the driver was pushing it off, passengers clapped and cheered at every attempt they made. It was a rare light-hearted moment!" Her laughter turned to tears as she told how their only son, Stefan, was taken at gunpoint while working in the field with some of the other farm workers, never to be seen again. With heavy heart the couple decided to leave the war-torn country and head for America.

The wrecked old car finally broke down in France, not many miles from Calais. The men pushed it to a safe place, collected their possessions and the four refugees continued on foot until they came across a bus to Calais Port.

"At least we don't have a goat to wrestle with," chuckled the incorrigible Donata.

They waited patiently for several hours before embarking on the ferry taking them the twenty-one or so miles across La Manche to England. As they neared Dover, they watched the outline of the White Cliffs emerge into view and sighed with relief that another stage of their long trek was ending.

After disembarking they were led to a large arrival area where overworked staff briefly scrutinized their documents and directed them out of the area where they boarded a coach for central London. Before parting company, Marc gave their companions an address in New York, where they planned to make their home with relatives.

"If you make it to New York, dear friends, be sure to call us," was the departing comment.

Zelda wept quietly as she waved her friends on their way.

"Such kind people! What would we have done without them?"

In London, Kristof and Zelda, as they now called each other, were exploited by rogue employers and found illegal work in a hotel where they slept in a cold attic room. Pay was minimal, work hours long and exhausting, but they were determined to save for flights to New York, to join thousands of Bosnians who headed there after escaping the genocide.

"We will never be able to afford flights to America at this rate," sighed Kristof as he counted out their meagre savings. "How can we obtain visas with no savings to back us up and with illegal passports? It's hopeless. We have to re-think our plans."

"We could go by ship!" shrieked Zelda in a moment of clear thinking.

"That's expensive too."

"I mean as crew, we could work on a cruise liner! There seem to be plenty of them around, we just have to find one calling at New York and work out how to stay there."

"That is a clever idea, dragi, but we must check it carefully."

Kristof spent most of his precious free time at the port watching, learning, noting America-bound liners, and planning.

It was several months before they obtained posts on a liner sailing to New York. They were excited, but apprehensive as a new adventure began for them. Kristof worked in the kitchen while Zelda, with her nursing experience, helped in the medical area. The hours were long and they saw little of each other as accommodation for male and female crew was strictly separate.

Their plan to jump ship was set in motion as crew were allowed twenty-four-hour shore leave.

"We have no visas, we are sure to be caught and deported," sighed the anxious Zelda.

Just then, an elderly passenger tripped on the gangway. Zelda, still in uniform, rushed forward to assist the distressed lady. Kristof helped his wife escort the patient to the first aid area where they remained until an ambulance arrived to transport her to hospital. In the chaos they found themselves outside the arrival area and free to move into the heart of the city.

The couple were awestruck at the splendour of New York and constantly strained their necks to see the tops of the gigantic buildings. They spent some time walking around the city, amazed at its size and grandeur. They located their friends Marc and Donata, whose relatives insisted that the young couple stay with them until they settled in the city of their dreams.

The four friends were overjoyed at being reunited. They sat together with their benevolent hosts well into the night, reminiscing on their travels through Europe, catching up with events since their parting in London and planning for the future.

Kristof walked the streets in search of work, taking any kind of illegal employment he could find. A woman walking ahead of him was unaware she had dropped her purse. Kristof ran after her to return it. She was so grateful for his honesty that she insisted he join her for coffee, during which his new friend introduced herself.

"I'm Rita, Rita Hampton. I'm a nurse and this is my

day off. I'm so grateful to you for returning my purse. I wasn't aware that I had dropped it. Thank you so much."

As they sat in the warmth of the café, Rita listened awestruck to his story of escape from Sarajevo and search for work.

"And now, here we are in New York, desperate for employment and accommodation. We cannot impose on our new friends for much longer. They have been kind to us, but we have to find our own way now that Zelda has fully recovered and is able to seek work."

"You sound like a hard-working, honest couple. Hey, let me make a call. Perhaps I can help you! Wait here, one moment please."

She returned, smiled broadly at the tense Kristof and said, "Take this address. Be there tomorrow, you and your wife, at two o'clock. Please be punctual. That will make a good impression."

She assured him accommodation and work could possibly be made available.

"Good luck."

And so, a new chapter began in the lives of Zelda and Kristof.

CHAPTER 16

"Why do we have to take such a crazy road trip in this atrocious weather? It is not safe for us or the child... so risky."

"I know honey, but you know that we have no choice but to take the agreed route and follow it precisely. I really wish it was different, really, I do... but..."

He became quiet, unable to voice his opinion, aware that their young detainee was awake and listening. They tried to limit the travelling to around 200 miles per day. Far too long for the girl to endure, he thought to himself as he drove along through Pennsylvania towards Ohio, where they made Cleveland the next stop. They arrived at Lake Erie as darkness descended, at a secluded area mapped out for them. There they rested up.

Some days later, their Midwest journey continued. They drove through Indiana towards Illinois on the by-pass system; "avoid Chicago at all costs," they had been instructed. Strong winds, falling temperatures and scattered snow showers developed into a full-blown storm, which forced them to hole up and seek shelter.

***

The squad working the case of the missing child were constantly harassed by their boss Harvey, who in turn was under pressure from the mayor and the superintendent to 'clear up this mess. It's not a good image for the city if we can't find this missing kid.' Extra officers were assigned to the case in an attempt to bring it to a head before the upcoming elections.

"It's got to be a revenge crime, not your normal kidnap or we would have had a demand by now." Harvey continued. "Who would want revenge on Brenda Mears or her empire? We seem to have discounted most of her staff and former employees, so who the hell is holding Lucy?"

Secretly he feared the girl may no longer be alive.

His greatly expanded team of officers gathered around while Detective Carr studied the whiteboard.

"George North? What would he have against Brenda? He seems to have a good job, conditions are excellent, his paycheque is healthy, and his personal life with Nora Kelly appears to be heading in the right direction. His sisters couldn't help in any way with his whereabouts. They have been out of touch now for several years. The flights he took on his time off were all to airports in New York, some to JFK, and some to Newark or La Guardia and once to MacArthur. Why different airports? So where did he go from there? The answer has to be in New York, that's for sure. He must have been picked up at these different airports—"

Harvey interrupted. "Get a team to each of these places and check CCTV cameras for those dates, that is, if they still have them. This enquiry is way over budget. My job is on the line if we don't come up with answers. Where is that kid? Also, as a matter of urgency we have to look more closely at employees of Mears. The guy, Barclay Ellis-Jones, where is he, where did he go after leaving Mears?"

As his team departed to their various tasks, Harvey called Officer Carr aside. "Carole, I've a sensitive issue to be tackled… you're the best person for this."

Detective Carr listened attentively to instructions, drew a sharp intake of breath and replied, "Ok, but wish me luck with this one."

Detective Carr met Brenda Mears in the privacy of her Lincoln Park home.

"Brenda, I have to ask you, I have been instructed by my boss to ask you a personal question, which I have to say must be investigated to ensure we cover all possibilities in finding Lucy. It's a sensitive question, but it has to be asked." With an intake of breath, Carr asked, "Who is Lucy's father? We have to locate him if for nothing else to eliminate him from enquiries."

Brenda sat bolt upright as if having been slapped.

"Sorry, Detective Carr, you have had a wasted journey. I swore never to reveal that to anyone, not until I have the opportunity to tell my daughter."

She stood up to show Carr to the door, but the detective remained seated.

"This information is crucial to enquiries. Lucy's father could be involved in her disappearance. At least let us eliminate him."

"Detective, Lucy's father does not know of her existence, and never will. Now, please leave that line of enquiry alone."

Carole Carr pleaded with Brenda for the information, but to no avail. Reluctantly, she returned to base to report to an irate Harvey of Brenda's unwillingness to co-operate.

"I thought that sending a female might have helped her open up about it. We have to get that information somehow. Try again. Perhaps her staff will know. Molly seems to have been there since Brenda was a baby, and Nora was her constant companion and perhaps her confidante. Also, check out birth records, although I doubt the father's name will be there."

Some days later both Carr and Harvey returned to Lincoln Park to speak to both Molly and Nora Kelly, the only people who could help reveal what they needed to know. Harvey sat in Molly's kitchen and explained the reason for her being questioned. She was visibly upset at the thought of divulging what was to her a trusted secret. Carr, meanwhile, found Nora busy in the laundry room. Both women were understandably shaken at the line of questioning.

"I can't betray Brenda. I made a solemn promise to her never to divulge that information, so I cannot tell you what you want to know."

"Molly, I fully understand your reticence and admire your loyalty, but surely Lucy's safety supersedes loyalty?"

Molly, red in the face, shook her head to confirm her decision. Nora, too, did not waver under pressure from Carr.

"I will never, ever be disloyal to Brenda over this, never."

In desperation, both women were brought together. Harvey again explained that they only wanted to eliminate the man.

"I will not tell you, detectives. I cannot break a promise made all those years ago," sobbed Molly.

"Nor will I," wept Nora. "Brenda is my employer, but she's also my friend."

"Ladies, you leave me no option then but to take you in and charge you with obstruction of justice."

Molly gasped and almost fell to the floor but for a hand grabbing her arm to prevent a fall.

"Stop right there, detectives!" hollered Brenda who had

heard sobbing and came to investigate. She witnessed Harvey's threat to the two women and arrived in time to prevent Molly from falling. She was furious.

"These women are not at fault and you know that. You are playing on their weakness and loyalty to me. They are only following my demands. I will not put them through this. Detectives, I will, under duress, give you the information you require. Then, I demand you leave my home. Now, come to my study."

She turned to her staff and hugged them both.

"Thank you for putting yourselves on the line for me. I'll give these people what they want. Nora, make your mom a strong cup of tea. You know she says it's the answer to everything."

Molly smiled at her employer's attempt to calm her.

Brenda led the detectives to her study and grudgingly gave them the information they so desperately wanted.

CHAPTER 17

Encouraging Dale Greer to drink up to drown his sorrows, a fellow drinker, with a comforting arm around his shoulders, said, "Sounds like you've had a tough time, buddy. Let me buy you another drink and you can tell me how a nice guy like you got such a bad deal."

"It's Cindy, you see, my wife... our lives have been ruined... and the kids... I can't even put a roof over their heads... they had to go live with her folks... ain't seen them in months. I ain't got two dimes to rub together, man. It's hopeless."

"Someone needs to cut you some slack, man. Maybe I could help you and your wife, Cindy. What a sweet name! That was my dear late sister's name. She died last year, I miss her so much, but, hey, maybe we could help your Cindy."

Dale's new friend explained he was part of a finance group and was sure he could lend Dale some cash. "Max $2,000 with an easy repayment scheme. You pay back what you can each week, minimum of five dollars. Think you could manage that, Dale?"

Assured that this would solve his immediate problems, Dale, through a fuzz of alcohol, wept into his drink and thanked his new friend, over and over until the guy said, "I have to make a call, buddy, stay around."

He returned sometime later with good news that Dale's loan had been approved and if he hung around for an hour or so, a courier would come with the dollars.

"Sorry I can't stay, Dale, I have a business meeting to get to. Les will be here as soon as he can. You enjoy your drink."

Les did indeed turn up with a package and showed the dollars to the grateful blubbering man who in his tipsy condition agreed to the terms. He signed on the dotted line little knowing what lay ahead.

Before very long, repayments became a nightmare for him and he found himself an unwilling, terrified participant in the disappearance of Lucy Mears. Like Clara Blake, he was "invited" to agree to an assignment that would cancel his debt. When questioned by officers he could not give a description of the moneylender as his mind had been fogged by alcohol. He did, however, remember the name of his drinking hole. Undercover officers were assigned to investigate the bar.

**

Feeling sorry for herself, Clara Blake sobbed quietly into her cheap drink.

"You upset, babe?" enquired a well-dressed, politely spoken guy. "How about I buy you a drink and you tell old Barclay here, all about it?"

Glad of company and a sympathetic ear, Clara through a blur of alcohol told an almost incoherent version of her financial nightmare and her wayward son.

"He's a good guy, my Samuel, just got in with the wrong company, wanted to help his mom out of some money problems... I've let him down... can't support my own kid... got no money for bail... poor Samuel, locked up in that hellhole cos of his bad mom."

Clara's tale spluttered out through her drunken state.

"Hell no, Clara. You don't mind me calling you Clara, do you, honey? Such a sweet name... it was my dear mother's name. She was a beautiful lady, just like you. Sadly, she passed away a year ago. I sure miss my mom. You're a good mom, I'm sure. I can see that in your pretty eyes; hell, you've just fallen on hard times. You know, Clara, I might be able to help you out and cut you some slack."

He offered her a way out of her difficulties. He was, he told her, a private financial advisor and was sure he could obtain a loan for her.

"Would two thousand dollars set you on your feet, Clara? You would have to repay a minimum each week of five dollars, more if you could afford it when times get better."

He excused himself to make a call and returned with news that $2,000 could be lent to her, once the paperwork was signed. Clara was elated.

"You're such a kind man Barclay, a credit to your mom."

"I have to go catch a flight, but stay here. My good friend Les from the firm will come here in an hour or so with some cash for you. Enjoy your drink. I'll have to rush off, sorry about that; I'd like nothing better than to spend more time with such a charming lady."

She agreed to wait for his colleague Les to arrive with the cash and a sheaf of papers. Sobbing quietly and drinking heavily, she signed the paperwork to complete the deal, having no idea of the amount of interest she had agreed to. Les took his leave of her.

***

Wracked with sorrow for himself, George North settled on a bar stool and began to drink. It wasn't long before he was well inebriated and fell from the stool with such a clatter it attracted the attention of the other drinkers.

"You ok, buddy?" asked a well-dressed, well-spoken man who helped him to his feet.

George mumbled his thanks, offered to buy his helper a drink and soon the pair were seated in a more comfortable area. George drank as if it were going out of fashion. His new friend sipped on his own drink while listening and encouraging George to talk about his worries.

"It's Nora, my sweet girl, that I'm thinking of. We've got plans and I don't want to let her down."

He continued to regale his friend with his financial problems. At times he was so incoherent that he had to repeat himself.

"If she can make a fortune, so can I," he mumbled.

"Who? Nora? Who is 'she'?"

"No, not my dear Nora, my employer, Brenda Mears. She's president of Mears Empire back in Chicago, palatial home, everything I want from life, dollars, dollars, dollars, you'd never imagine one person having so much… life's unfair."

On hearing the name Brenda Mears, Barclay drew a sharp intake of breath and became utterly transfixed on the guy's dreadful story of his life and work with the one person he had sworn to get even with. Memories flooded back from his time there.

George rambled on, unaware that the probing from his new drinking buddy, which elicited many details from him about his employer, only rekindled the man's dislike of the woman who had the nerve to spurn his advances. He was particularly interested in hearing more about the daughter who was only a young kid when he left Mears.

"Clever kid, no doubt about it," mumbled the almost incoherent, inebriated, pathetic human being. "Talented musician, has been since a very young age, one of those child prodigies, only fifteen years of age, plays the cello like a true professional... plays in her school orchestra." He sobbed even more at the memory. "Hell, I promised to take my Nora to the kid's concert in Chicago next week."

He encouraged George to talk more about his finances. George wept when the guy told him that perhaps he could help.

"Your lucky day, buddy, when you fell off that stool." *Fate, in more ways than one*, he thought to himself. He explained that he was part of a large financial organization, which could lend him a few dollars. "Max $2,000, buddy, with an easy payback scheme, to get you on your feet."

"Enough to get me my computer equipment and set me on the right road?"

"Sure, buddy, it sure would help you win back your dear Nora. Such a sweet name, Nora. That was my dear mom's name; she died a year ago. I sure miss my mom. Let me go make a call."

Arrangements were made for George to be given the cash. All he had to do was stay where he was and enjoy his drink. Barclay Jones mentally took note of the proposed venue for Lucy Mears' concert, then arranged to have the money brought to George by a courier.

"It won't be me bringing your dollars, George. I've a flight to catch. Stay here and my colleague Les will find you."

Pleased with his success in snaring another pitiful

victim, he left the seedy surroundings to return home to wash off the stink of the evening.

Well out of his mind with drink and elated by his good fortune, George willingly signed his name to the paper proffered to him by Les who turned up showing George the package containing more dollars than he had seen in some time. George put the package safely in his inside pocket and staggered back to his hotel, unable to believe his good fortune, and longed to be back home with Nora.

CHAPTER 18

Disaster struck the trio in the form of sickness. Lucy, normally a healthy robust child, was the first to succumb to a violent sickness and ague, causing grave concern for her minders. Her female captor, a former nurse, ministered to the sick girl, dispensed medication and cooled her fevered brow. She comforted the frightened, restless girl, soothing and calming her young patient during the height of the fever. Lucy moaned in her sleep and constantly called for "Mama, call Mama".

Fearing she too might become ill, she instructed her partner on how to care for them. When she did develop the illness, he coped as best he could in nursing them both. Knowing her previous medical history, he was concerned about her fragility. Before long, he too became sick and the trio were at the mercy of nature as they parked up in a desolate, remote place.

Lucy slowly recovered and became aware of moaning from the other room. She struggled through to where she found the female captor fevered and agitated, calling out in a strange language. Instinct told Lucy to tend to her. She tenderly proffered cool sips of water as she wiped the fevered face of the sick lady. Her partner slept fitfully by her side. Lucy felt frightened at the thought of what might happen if her captors became much sicker. It was many days before the group had fully recovered enough to take stock of their dire situation.

"We must move on as best we can. Our water supply is running low and I have missed the deadline to report to Boss," moaned the weak man.

"We are far too frail to travel further," she replied. "We need to rest up properly somewhere safe and restock our supplies."

They cautiously travelled some distance and found a motel complex near a small grocery store. The manager was amazed at the mode of transport of the sickly-looking guy who checked in and mumbled about having to visit a sick relative, stating he had no other vehicle. He was reluctant to involve the hotelier in conversation. Once more Lucy was secretly carried to the motel room where the trio spent several more days in recovery. Much later than arranged the man made the call.

"You are late!"

"Boss, we have all been sick." He then related events and was given a change of route that he was to take.

Refuelled and stocked up, they set off once more on their grim journey. They travelled slowly, covered less ground and rested often.

"Please, please, Call Mama," a weary voice called again in desperation.

"I know, honey, this is hard for you, for us all, but soon we will reach our destination and you will understand more."

The exhausted trio journeyed on through Wisconsin to St. Croix River, where they stayed for some time at Stillwater, Minnesota.

***

Kip O'Rourke, one of Harvey's team, took in every word his boss related concerning the case of missing Lucy

Mears. The unfolding events intrigued him. He held his superior in high esteem, but as for Carole Carr, he had very different feelings. Having been shortlisted for promotion and hoping to be Harvey's right-hand man, he was incensed when Carr was promoted over him and consequently found it difficult to work with her. She was totally unaware of her colleague's dislike of her, believing his congratulatory remarks to be genuine. He watched and waited, hoping she would make an error of judgement, which he could use to discredit her, such was his resentment.

"I'm on your tail, lady," he murmured to himself. "One false move…"

He was a devious character with a nasty streak. His best buddy was a long-term high school friend, a reporter, to whom he fed snippets of information sure in the knowledge that nothing could be traced back to him. For a tidy sum, he planned to give his buddy the big one: news of Lucy Mears whenever the abduction ended, as it surely would. During lunch with his friend he offloaded his feelings about Carole Carr, his bitterness spewing from his mouth as he let his emotions vent.

"A few discreet bugging devices are called for here, Kip boy. Tell me where you want them hidden. I know a guy who's an expert at this sort of thing, does it often for me."

"Sonny, you kept that quiet!"

Kip's buddy Sonny was fearless when it came to planting bugs, fitting tracing devices to cars and generally messing with surveillance equipment, sometimes working alone, sometimes with a trusted accomplice whom he named "slipper" due to the guy's ability to slip in, fix bugs and slip out without detection. Sonny successfully planted devices in Harvey's office and Carr's private vehicle. He deliberately did not inform Kip of the exact location of the gadgets as he knew his friend was a weak character, who, if confronted, would spill the beans and land him in trouble.

CHAPTER 19

Barclay Jones travelled to Chicago to attend Lucy's school concert.

Unwilling to risk being spotted by Brenda Mears, he waited until the last moment to claim a seat at the back of the hall. His mission was simply to spot the Mears kid. Identification was essential for the plan forming in his mind. Proud parents were permitted to use cameras on condition there was to be no flash photography, which suited Barclay Jones, as he recorded Lucy Mears' solo performance.

Sure has talent, he thought to himself.

From his distant position he spotted Brenda Mears. Seeing the woman was enough to reawaken his hatred of her, spurring him to plan his revenge. As intermission was announced he made to leave the hall promptly, satisfied with the evening's results. Another spectator sitting nearby also rose to leave. They reached the door at the same time. Barclay Jones turned, a look of recognition on his smiling face.

"Hey, how are you? It's been a long time!"

"Hey, how are you, Barclay?"

The two exited the building, renewing acquaintances and chatting as they went along. Unknown to them at this point, this chance encounter was to launch a series of events that would have consequences reverberating well beyond the city of Chicago.

"Have you eaten?" enquired Barclay.

Together, the duo headed for a quiet restaurant that his companion recommended.

"It's off the beaten track so we shouldn't be disturbed by hordes from the school."

During the course of the evening, encouraged by the ambience, the flow of alcohol and completely trusting his fellow diner, Barclay revealed his loathing of Brenda Mears and his wish to exact revenge on her.

"How to make her suffer, that's the challenge for me," he mused.

As they chatted, he told his companion about his life, his time in prison and his loan scheme, causing raucous laughter.

"I like that, you old scoundrel! Hey, I might just have a suggestion for you to consider."

And so, the pair hatched a plot that was to involve some of Barclay's victims of his loan fraud scheme, cause hours of police time and, unknown to them at that moment, have repercussions reaching almost to the White House itself.

"Our main co-ordinator will be your George North guy. Agree?"

"Sure. He will have no choice but to co-operate," answered Barclay.

"He can set in motion the first stage in our plan, which will give Brenda Mears a taste of suffering she never imagined could exist in her cosseted life. Leave the details with me for a few days. Contact me directly on this private number only. Do not use my name, ever, or reveal it to anyone, understand? You call me Boss, from now on in, Boss."

"Hey, I like that," agreed the animated rogue. "Ok, Boss!"

As they parted company, Barclay Jones, with a spring in his step, thanked his lucky stars for his chance meeting with an old friend.

"Boss, yeah, I like it!"

His newly found conspirator returned home and mulled over the details of a plan to bring chaos into the life of the president of Mears Empire. Barclay called Boss as instructed and was invited to stay at headquarters to discuss plans. He was flabbergasted at the opulence of the place and stood in awe as he studied the splendour of Boss's home.

"Listen up… this is what we do," began Boss. "I'll fund this project and have great pleasure in doing so. These are the people from your contacts whom we can make use of: George North, we have already mentioned, Dale Greer and Clara Blake. From what you told me about them they should be amenable to our request. This is what each will do… if they carry out instructions and keep their mouths shut, cancel their debt… I'll refund your losses."

Boss relayed in detail the plan to cause maximum chaos for Brenda Mears and continued:

"My people here will be heavily involved in all stages of the plan. Your two business buddies will be needed as well. You will all be well rewarded but swear them to secrecy on the pain of death."

He was convinced Boss was well able to carry out such a threat.

The stunned conspirator could hardly believe his turn of fortune. He arrived home to brief his fellow rogues and swear them to secrecy, spelling out the consequences if they dared breathe a word to anyone.

"Looks like you'll be doing a bit of flying again, buddy," he said to the exuberant Les.

Subsequent visits to Boss finalized details of the heinous crime about to be perpetrated.

"It's up to George North now to keep his cool and set it all in motion when the opportunity arises. Let's drink to the success of the greatest plot ever imagined!"

CHAPTER 20

Ross S. Witherspoon kissed his wife and kids and set off on the campaign trail.

"Be good to Mom, you guys, see you soon."

Linda-Mae, his wife, taught kindergarten; an elegant lady, refined, articulate, an asset on any aspiring politician's arm, called after him, "See you Saturday, honey."

She planned to join him for a weekend of campaigning once her parents arrived to take on the task of looking after the kids. Ross S. Witherspoon smelt victory in his attempt to become his party presidential nomination. His entire life centred on politics. His late grandfather lived and breathed politics and had a willing pupil in young Ross for whom he had great plans.

"You can be anything you want, Ross, if you're ambitious enough. Hey, you could even be president of the United States if you had a mind to," mused the former politician.

He never tired of telling his young grandson how Abraham Lincoln was a home-state nomination in 1860, how the electoral voters from the state of Illinois, with near half its population located in Chicago-dominated Cook County, were a factor in the win for Kennedy over Richard Nixon, and how, in his own opinion, the first black president would sure as hell have Chicago connections.

"A great city, son, one to be proud of, needs good leadership; you can be that guy, you have to work your way up the political ladder and where better to start than here, where folk know you, know your family and know your old grandpappy who was the best mayor ever elected, even if I say so myself."

"You were, grandpappy, you sure were!" exclaimed the besotted boy who never tired of hearing the old man's memories, which fired his passion to be the best of politicians.

"Don't forget, Ross, our ancestor signed the Declaration of Independence."

This fact had never been proven, but old Mayor Witherspoon clung to it as gospel, set in stone.

Young Ross S. Witherspoon was taken on a trip to Washington. The impressionable lad, mesmerized by the whole experience, stood at the Lincoln Memorial as Grandpa read aloud to him from the inscription there. Hairs stood up on the back of his neck, his young eyes moist from an emotion he had never experienced before. Capitol Hill, the White House, the splendour of D.C. became for him the driving force to make politics his life. His ultimate aim: Washington D.C.

He was a handsome, fine-featured man, tall, elegant, smartly dressed, a man who could, and did, break the hearts of many from an early age when he discovered his prowess with the ladies. He made heads turn when he entered a room; women were drawn to him like bees around a honey pot. He used them and left them.

He had inherited a legacy from his grandfather specifically stating it was to be used to further his political career. He knew any campaign would require massive funding to elect him to public office. As a single man he also knew his image would be enhanced by the acquisition of a beautiful wife. His sights were centred on that and on amassing funds for his campaigns.

He dated several women in his youth and was introduced to a young, gregarious lady who was heir to the growing Mears Empire. He became determined to develop his relationship with her over the years, seeing dollar signs as each date progressed. Several months into the relationship, Brenda Mears, besotted with her handsome, ambitious suitor who lavished attention on her, making her the envy of every woman who attended glittering functions, announced to her lover that she was pregnant. She was unprepared for his reaction, thinking marriage and children would cement their affair.

"Pregnant? No, this can't be! You crazy woman, this is too soon for my plans right now. I need to do things in the right order. Get rid of it. You foolish woman. You won't trick me into marriage I am not ready for this."

With that, he stormed off, scaring Brenda with his sudden change of attitude. All further attempts to contact him proved futile. Her calls went unanswered, his staff instructed never to reply to her pleas for his time. A bewildered Brenda, accepting the relationship was over, relied on her father, Molly and Nora to sustain her through her pregnancy. She swore them to secrecy.

"Never, ever, reveal the name of my child's father. I will be the one to tell the child in my own good time."

Linda-Mae Sheringham always wanted to teach, much to the disappointment of her parents who had hoped their only child would follow them in a law career.

"You can do better than that, honey," they pleaded.

Linda-Mae followed her heart and qualified as a teacher. She loved the buzz of working with young people, filling their minds with as much knowledge as they craved with their unending questions and comments. She enjoyed watching her charges soak up information like sponges. She returned home each evening exhausted but satisfied with her day's work.

She met Ross S. Witherspoon at her parents' home when they held a dinner party to introduce some friends to a political acquaintance seeking re-election as senator. He had brought with him a young high-flyer who hoped someday to stand for election himself, his mentor promising to introduce him to influential people who could assist his campaign.

Ross dated Linda-Mae for several years as he climbed the political ladder and to the delight of her parents announced their engagement. Within a few months, a lavish wedding took place, paid for by her parents who were more than comfortably off, a fact that had not gone unnoticed by the groom.

Linda-Mae, now Mrs. Witherspoon, was a dutiful politician's wife, who accompanied him to meetings, fundraising events and various gatherings. She was not blind to her husband's charming attraction to other women and kept him on a tight leash. After handing over her two children to the safekeeping of her parents, she joined her husband on what was hoped to be a step nearer election for the power-hungry man.

When he was seen to be a serious contender for presidential nomination, his mentor, Steve Wilkes, asked him outright if there was anything in his background that could come back and bite him.

"Squeaky clean, Steve," he laughed. "There's nothing to worry about; happily married to a beautiful lady, two great sons, good family pedigree, no one can dish any dirt on Ross S. Witherspoon's character."

"Good to hear that, but we have to be sure of these things. You know our culture with its tendency to mistrust politicians. It's so ingrained in society to be suspicious of those in power. If you want to serve a full term, things have to be clear cut."

"Steve, you fret too much. I plan to be an honest president of unquestionable integrity."

"You'll be the first then," muttered his mentor under his breath.

Steve Wilkes was a shrewd man, never taking any client at face value until he had enquired thoroughly into the credentials of his runner. He employed a private detective to do the tedious groundwork for him, a search that in the case of Ross S. Witherspoon was to have catastrophic results. He regularly employed an ex-con, a shady character, but one who got results for him. Steve never enquired as to methods used; he just paid the guy for information.

Les Soubry first met Steve Wilkes when the latter visited a client in prison. Les was working in the library when Steve passed and said, "Hi."

The two got into conversation and Steve took the opportunity to develop a business deal with the con whom he perceived to be someone who would relish the job he had in mind.

"Want to earn a few bucks, buddy?"

"Can always use a few bucks in here. What you got in mind?"

"Need a guy monitored... you interested?"

"Like a spy thing? James Bond stuff?"

"Something like that. You know 'Crazy Pike', they call him?"

"Yeah, crazy by name and crazy by nature." Les laughed at his own joke.

"Well, I need someone to report to me on the guy. Just

listen for any mention of the robbery he committed… we're trying to locate the loot he's hidden. Big reward offered… you'll be well rewarded for any relevant information."

So began regular spy missions for the bored con who revelled in his newfound wealth.

"Hey Soubry, where'd you get money for smokes?" he was asked by fellow inmates.

"My poor aunt Cristobel died and left me some dosh, not much. My lawyer sends me some dollars, invests the rest for me for when I'm outta here."

The story sounded plausible enough and allowed Les freedom to spend his few dollars without too many questions being asked. On release from prison, he occasionally continued clandestine work for Steve Wilkes.

"You ready for another assignment, Les?"

"I am that," said the ex-con seeing dollar signs.

"There's a politician I want you to keep your ears open about. Any mention of him, however small, let me know."

Les Soubry began frequenting various bars where he knew journalists hung out, hoping he might pick up some useful information since politics was high on the agenda on the run-up to the presidential nominations.

Ross S. Witherspoon threw himself headlong into the road to the White House and announced his plan to run for office. Caucuses were traditionally lively events where local party members gathered to nominate their candidate and many fell under the spell of this charming man. It was no surprise when voters cast their votes at the primaries and Ross S. Witherspoon, nominee for president, was announced at a national party convention. His nomination campaign won him the trophy; delegates flocked behind the charismatic man, seeing in him hope for a bright future for the party and for themselves. A lucrative career beckoned those who could ingratiate themselves with the great man himself. He stood there, a proud man, glowing in the adulation of the crowd, holding firmly the hand of the would-be first lady.

"Now, let's get the real work done. The presidential campaign begins in earnest."

The crowd was euphoric as they pledged their allegiance, and their dollars, to their champion.

***

Les Soubry, drinking in a dimly lit and crowded bar, overheard part of a conversation between two men at the next table who were discussing the forthcoming election. They then moved on to discuss the Mears investigation. Les picked up snippets of the conversation: "bombshell... get it at the right moment when he takes questions..."

"You sure about this, Sonny? It's way too big to get wrong. You sure your snooper looked into the background of the guy?"

"Kip, trust me on this. My buddy knew someone from the guy's past, used to live near him in Chicago, knew his family. This sure checks out."

"Hey you, what you think you're doing, listening to private conversations?" said one of the men looking straight at Les.

Les turned back to his drink as Kip O'Rourke and Sonny Woods left the bar.

Near thing that, he thought to himself.

"Do you think that creep heard anything in there?" asked Kip of Sonny as they drove off.

"No, he looked so out of it with drink he won't remember his own name!"

Les arranged to meet briefly with Steve at the back of the venue while the aspiring politician continued with his speech. He briefed him on what he had heard.

"I thought you'd want this news ASAP."

Steve was dumbfounded at what Les had to report.

"Owe you big, but keep this to yourself. Tell no one. You understand?"

He handed Les more dollars than the ex-con had ever seen, ensuring the spy would indeed keep the information to himself in the hope that more of the same came his way.

The politician finished his speech. Steve stood at the back of the hall, staring at the man he had mentored and guided to this moment. *I'll have to speak to him after the question session.* He sighed as he moved nearer the podium, hoping against hope that somehow Les had picked things up wrong, but knowing in his heart that what he had just heard was correct.

His speech finished, Ross S. Witherspoon immersed himself in the idolization of the faithful. Like a peacock, he paraded among his followers. His mentor guided him back to the podium.

"Time to take some questions, Ross."

CHAPTER 21

Having convinced Brenda Mears that the attempted break-in at her home was nothing to be concerned about, George saw off the errand-boys sent to his employer's estate. He read the note he had been given. The envelope contained a disturbing picture of Nora, leaving no doubt in his mind that harm would come to her if he failed to repay his loan. He had no option but to comply with the demands. Also in the envelope was a copy of the agreement he had signed in his drunken state. Highlighted were the consequences of late or non-payment, the reality of which petrified him. The rate of interest shocked him.

"God help me," he sobbed quietly.

He quickly sent off an immediate payment to the bank number he had been given. This gave him only temporary respite. Before long he had no funds. He was in serious trouble. He sold his precious computer equipment, telling Nora it had gone for servicing. His morose demeanour concerned her. She interpreted his reticence and emotional detachment as lack of interest in their relationship. He ignored all attempts to communicate. He lost weight and no longer cared about his appearance. Molly and Nora were convinced he was seriously ill.

On a few days' leave, he flew to New York, informing Nora that he would be attending a computer course. Arriving at JFK, he was met by a courier and driven several miles to an imposing gated mansion. He was met by a man he thought he had seen somewhere before.

"We meet again, George. You remember me, don't you? I helped you up from a bar stool."

"I've a dim memory of something like that," he stuttered.

Barclay Jones continued. "We brought you here, George, to discuss your financial difficulty. You seem to have a problem with repaying the $2,000 we lent you."

The agitated man attempted to reply.

"Sorry, didn't fully understand what I was getting into... I must have been dipso... just need a bit more time, sir... I'll get the money."

"How, George? You've no cash. You sold your computer, didn't you? Where do you think you're going to get money? Nora, perhaps? Brenda Mears?"

Poor George almost burst into tears. Barclay Jones continued.

"Don't get upset. We've brought you here to offer you a way out... got a job for you... do it well and the slate will be wiped clean. You interested?"

George visibly relaxed.

"Sure, I'll do anything... what's this place? Who is 'we'?"

"You'll be told on a need-to-know basis. Listen up: you will be taken upstairs to meet Boss, who will explain everything to you."

Boss briefed George on the assignment. This was to be his only meeting with the mysterious Boss. He listened intensely; fear crushed him as he took in the enormity of the task.

"Hey, I can't do that! Not Lucy..." he protested. "Lucy trusts me. I won't take part in this crazy idea."

"Yeah, you will do this, Mr. North. Think about it,

you will be debt free. If you refuse, on your own head be it. Yeah, Lucy trusts you, so it should be relatively easy. It's payback time."

The alternative was explained to him. His beloved Nora would be in serious danger if he failed to comply.

"Oh hell, oh God, don't harm her, please."

"No one will be harmed, George, if you follow my instructions. I'm afraid you can't leave here until you agree. Think. Do this one thing and you'll not only have your loan paid in full, you'll be given enough dollars to set you and Nora up in business. I'll give you time to consider."

George was led to a room where he was locked in. The room was near the top of the building. Although it was comfortable and well appointed, there was no television or phone. He was isolated. Enticing meals and drinks were brought to him. *Could live like this with Nora*, he thought. *Maybe, just maybe, I should do what they ask...*

Barclay Jones arrived some time later.

"Have you had time to consider your position? Boss will make it worth your while. You won't meet Boss again; I'm your link man now."

"As long as no harm comes to Lucy, she's just a kid."

"You have Boss's word on that."

Specific instructions were explained to George. He was horrified.

"Return to Chicago now... no crazy ideas or you'll never see your darling Nora again. Alf, here will explain what will happen to her if you breathe a word of this to anyone."

George shuddered as Alf detailed his graphic plan for Nora.

"Don't... don't touch her... ok... I'll do it."

George returned to Chicago a broken man. He scarcely

spoke. He was too scared in case he let something slip. A few days after his return, Nora, shopping in the mall, was pushed to the ground and had her purse stolen. She screamed in pain. Shoppers came to her assistance. Some hours later she arrived home with her arm in a cast. That evening George received a text. It read: "A warning." Any thoughts he had of reneging on his mission faded as he comforted Nora.

"The guy came from nowhere, pushed me to the ground and grabbed my purse. I tried to hold on to it, but he pulled furiously. If I'd let him take it I might not be in this sorry state."

She sobbed in her lover's arms.

George made several more trips to New York. On each visit, more instructions were issued. Nora continued to believe he was attending computer courses. He was given a top-of-the-range computer by whoever Boss was. His driver, Les, spoke sparingly and would not reveal anything about Boss.

"Never met anyone there except Barclay. Don't know anything about Boss."

Back home, Brenda asked George to collect Lucy from school to allow Nora to visit the dentist. He hurried to the privacy of his room and with heavy heart made a call, saying, "It's on!"

CHAPTER 22

Clara Blake made her way to the Correction Centre to visit her son. *Hate this journey. That place scares the hell outta me. Never know what you're gonna see...won't forget last time... that fight... two guys almost killed each other... wish to hell Sammy was outta there.* She waited in the visitor area. Her son shuffled in, escorted by prison wardens.

"Hey Mom, good you've come. Didn't think you'd be back after last time."

"What the heck happened to your face, son?"

"Nothing, Mom, bumped into a door, wasn't lookin' where I was going."

"Don't you stonewall me, Samuel Blake. I know a beating when I see one. God knows, I had plenty from your father. Who did that?"

"Keep your voice down, Mom," he replied, looking furtively around. "I'm good, I'm ok, just some guy thought I looked at him kinda funny. No big deal. These things happen in here."

"Son, I wish to hell you were home. This ain't no place for a boy."

"Mom, you worry too much. I'll be out soon and I promise I'm gonna make it up to you. I'll get a job, I'll—"

"Yeah, Sammy, heard it all before."

Clara returned home to find a letter in her mailbox. It read: "A warning." Enclosed was a picture of her boy, which scared her so much she began to howl. Enclosed also was a copy of the agreement she had signed in the bar. Clara panicked.

She had missed two payments, had a false sense of security and put it to the back of her mind, until now. Highlighted was the rate of interest for late payment.

"Hell no. Oh my boy!"

She quickly sent off what she could afford, several dollars short of the expected payment. Some days later, she had a visit from two men. The terrified woman had no option but to admit them to her house.

"Clara, good to meet you again. You remember me? The guy at the bar who saved your butt? Gave you $2,000. Remember?"

Indeed, she remembered, but the smooth-talking, polite man she vaguely recalled no longer seemed so friendly.

"Umm, yeah, sort of…"

"Alf here wants to show you a few pictures of your cute kid."

Alf laid out four pictures of Samuel: bruised, his left eye closed, his face almost unrecognizable.

She screamed in pain. "Leave my kid alone. I'll get your damn money."

"Now, Clara, calm down. You know you ain't got a spare dime. We're here to help you out. Got a little job for you. You do it well and little Sammy here will serve his sentence in peace and we'll wipe the slate clean… no more repayments."

He laid out clearly the task in hand.

"That's it?" she said incredulously. "You want me to hide a kid here for a few days and my boy will be ok and I don't have to pay no more money?"

"That's all that's to it, Clara, but you can't breathe a word to anyone or let the kid be seen. Don't let anyone into the house while you're looking after the kid. If you do, or mess up, well, Sammy boy…"

He made menacing signs with his hands, clear enough for her to fully understand. The two men left. Clara burst into tears, clutching the pictures they had left as a reminder.

***

Dale Greer, having lost all his savings after a bank meltdown, had his house foreclosed. His family moved in with his in-laws. He managed to find some menial, low-paid work and rented a cheap apartment, but was soon unable to pay his rent. The proprietor sent him packing. His wife, Cindy, found him after trawling one bar to another, hauled him outside where she berated him for his appearance.

"Look at you! An apology for a human being. You were supposed to be finding work to provide for us. My folks can't keep us forever. You disgust me."

She returned to her parents' home worried sick about the future.

Dale sought solace the only way he could. While drinking in a bar, he was approached by the two loan sharks who took him aside, showed him pictures of his wife, leaving him in no doubt as to what would happen to her should he fail to repay his loan. He blubbered like a baby.

"Hey, man, no need to be upset, we're here to help you out. We have a job for you; do it right and we'll not expect any more payments from you… wipe the slate clean… what could be easier?"

His task was explained to him in detail. He was to collect a kid, escort her by long-haul bus to New York to a safe house. He was to tell no one about this mission.

"In case you think of double crossing us…" Alf held up a picture of Cindy, leaving it with the terrified man as he and his accomplice left the bar.

Dale waited several days for instructions to be given regarding his mission, which involved hours of tedious travel. After returning from his task, which cleared him of burdensome debt, he received several visits from police officers. The strain of lying to them to protect his wife and family proved too much for the distraught man. Dale could no longer cope. He left his makeshift camp and walked deeper into the woods, rope in hand. Relentless rain battered his broken body. He was unaware of anything but his guilt.

"Forgive me, Cindy."

Officers sent to interview Dale Greer one more time could not locate him. His makeshift camp in the woods was intact, his tent and belongings left untouched. They asked around the local bars; no one had seen the dishevelled hobo, although they did know to whom they were referring.

"He's usually in here every evening, propping up the bar," reported a bar owner. "He's not been in for two, maybe three nights now. I presumed he'd moved on."

Local police were put on alert to extend the search and bring him in for questioning. Several days later, a couple exercising their dog in the woods came across a gruesome sight.

His distraught wife, Cindy, identified Dale Greer's body.

"I never thought it would come to this; I never stopped

loving him, you know. It was just, well, the kids had to have a future and Dale couldn't provide that. It wasn't his fault, detective. Greedy bankers are to blame for my husband lying in that morgue, as sure as if they had strung him to that tree themselves. He was a proud man, worked hard in the textile industry, earned well and saved hard for our future."

Carole Carr comforted the distressed lady. "Take your time, Cindy, you need to talk this through and unburden yourself."

"You're right. I couldn't talk much to my folks. Guess I was too ashamed and they were doing their best for us, but I'll never forget the day Dale told me of the collapse of the bank we had trusted all our married life."

"'Honey,' he wept on my shoulder. 'Honey, it's a disaster for us, all our savings, every damn dollar has gone.'"

Through tears, Cindy continued.

"Ma'am, he was a broken man, he aged overnight. The next few months were pure hell. I watched the man I loved crumble and weep like a baby. He couldn't eat, sleep or think straight. I had to be the strong one in the partnership and take charge of everything. My job as a dental receptionist didn't cover the mortgage repayments for long; we had to eat, other bills had to be paid, the kids needed shoes. Our precious house was repossessed, we sold what we could; we would have been better giving it away for all we got for our beautiful furniture. Vultures seem to sense when you are desperate and at your lowest ebb; people were offering ridiculously low prices, knowing we had no choice but to take their dollars.

"My folks gave the boys and me a home; we hoped it would be temporary. Dale opted to stay on in New York and look for work. He found a cheap place to live. After a few months, I came back to meet up with him and was shocked at his changed appearance. He earned enough to pay his rent but used the rest for drink. detective Carr, before this mess Dale never drank much, but he had totally lost it."

Cindy sobbed for some time, before continuing.

"I went like a crazy woman, berating him like hell, so now I'm suffering guilt. I should have taken him back to my folks' place to sort him out, but I was so angry. Now I've got to live with that, knowing the kids will never see their daddy again."

Carole Carr listened sympathetically to the distraught widow.

"From what we can gather, Cindy, Dale could no longer afford to stay in his rented accommodation, and the owner was objecting to his drinking, so he set up a campsite in the woods. He got himself involved with rogue moneylenders that he told us about when we interviewed him and thanks to Dale we have arrested one of the culprits. Your husband seemed to have been a good man, Cindy; don't beat yourself up about this. It just got too much for him."

"Can I take him home for burial?"

"We will release his body to you in the next few days and we can arrange for counselling for you and your family."

Detective Carr hugged the tragic woman before parting company.

CHAPTER 23

Carr sat with Harvey in his office, trying to assimilate the stunning news from Brenda Mears.

"This is big stuff, what do we do? We can't go public, it could ruin an innocent man."

"That is, if he is innocent," replied Carr.

They discussed their options. Harvey was unusually perplexed as to how to proceed.

"How can we keep this quiet from the rest of the squad? The mayor and superintendent are on our backs to get this case solved, and quickly. I hate concealing stuff from the others, but it's too big to risk having some bigmouth telling his mate in the pub or pillow talk with the wife or mistress or anyone else for that matter. It's a mess. We'll have to speak to the super and the mayor."

"Could we ask them to keep a lid on it till we've had time to locate the guy and eliminate him?"

"At the moment, Carr, we keep this strictly between ourselves. We need thinking time."

Meanwhile, two undercover agents settled themselves at the bar of the Water Vole and sipped from pints of ghastly beer while surreptitiously noting the customers as they came in for their drinking sessions. As the evening wore on, the volume in the bar increased; a few arguments developed, alternating between loud chatter and raucous laughter. The agents, as instructed, began a conversation about the state of their finances.

"I'm getting into deep debt. These kids of mine demand the latest gizmos, won't wear anything unless it has a designer label, run up bills on their mobile phones and expect me to pay up."

He put his head in his hands and continued.

"I can't bring myself to tell Joanne that I've lost my job. I go out in the morning as if I'm going to work and hole out somewhere until it's time to come home. It's stressing me out, don't know what I'll do at the end of the month when there's no paycheque."

"Hell, man, you sure are in a mess, worse than I thought. What are you going to do? I can't even help you out, buddy. Beth's surgery emptied the bank book, sorry, mate."

"Can't think of any way out, can't try for a loan with no regular paycheques to back it up; who will lend *me* money?"

The two continued to commiserate, feigned drunkenness, got louder as they consoled each other and agreed to go home, sleep on it and meet the next day, "same time, same place". They were about to leave when they became aware of a man standing at their side.

"Sorry, guys, couldn't help overhearing your conversation."

"Who the hell are you?" mumbled the "drunken" agent.

"I could be your saviour, buddy. I couldn't help but listen to you, this place is so packed out there's nowhere to stand without hearing other folk's conversation. Hey, maybe I could help. I know a reputable moneylender who might be able to get you an instant loan, small number of repayments till you get yourself sorted out."

Unknown to the guy, one of the agents had switched

on a tape and was recording the entire conversation.

"Tell me more," stuttered the drunk.

"Come over here where it's quieter and I'll explain how it works."

The two drunks, holding each other up, staggered to a quiet corner where their new friend explained how the distraught guy could borrow up to $2,000, paid back at $10 a week and more anytime he had a bit spare.

"Hey, let me make a call."

He returned to his victims.

"Meet here, same time tomorrow, for a courier to bring the cash. His name is Les. Sorry, guys, I can't stay around and talk, I've a flight to catch. Hey, it's been good talking to you. I'm sure things will work out just fine for you, buddy."

Faking tears of relief, he grabbed his rescuer by the arm, offered to buy him a drink, thanked him profusely, and wept on the guy's shoulder. The man called it a night and left the pub, glad to be out of the hellhole of human misery.

After some time, the colleagues left arm in arm, staggered along the street to avoid suspicion and when they were sure the coast was clear, "sobered up" and got into a crap car parked some way off.

"Did you record it then?"

"Got it! Now we're nearer to unmasking the loan sharks and their outfit."

The following evening as planned, the scruffy agents, beer splashed about their clothes, returned staggering to the Water Vole, pretended to drink several pints and waited.

A full hour passed before the expected courier appeared, beckoned them over to a corner table and produced a bulky, brown package. He opened it just enough to show the dollar bills inside, taking care to conceal it from view of the public.

"You're one lucky guy. We don't give these specials to just everyone. There's 2,000 bucks here. You sign right here, buddy, and your troubles are over."

The drunken agent continued to role-play, fawning over his new buddy and offering him a few drinks in gratitude.

"Hey, man, you've no idea how things will change now. My sweet Joanne will be—"

Just then, a shadow fell over the trio as two officers of the law approached the guy and cuffed him before he had time to draw breath.

As he was led away, he spat at the two agents, yelled profanities and struggled with the arresting policemen. Officers cuffed Lesley Jake Soubry, put him in the back of a police car, read him his Miranda and drove him to the precinct where he was interviewed by Harvey.

"I want my lawyer," demanded the prisoner.

"You got something you need a lawyer for, then?"

Les kept quiet, not exactly sure where this interview would take him, wondering too what this detective knew of his dubious life.

"So, sir," began Harvey. "I see you're a jailbird, one of our regulars."

"Don't mean nothing, 'cos I've done time. It don't mean I've committed a felony now."

"That's true, sir," continued the detective. "So, tell me, what's your involvement in the abduction of Lucy Mears?"

"Hey, you can't pin that on me! I know nothing about that kid. Ok, I admit I've helped a guy out a few times, nothing illegal like, but no way am I into this crap."

"You've heard of Lucy Mears, then?"

"Sure, hasn't everyone? The kid's picture's in every newsstand, on every TV channel. Who's not to know of Lucy Mears?"

"Les, you don't mind me calling you Les? Let's keep this kinda friendly, then you can go home. You see my problem. This kid's missing. Her mom's mega rich, willing to pay big bucks for the kid's return. You could earn a bit of bread, mate, I mean loads… just help me out here."

Les fell for the soft approach, thinking how he'd love to get his hands on enough cash to take off somewhere and have a good life.

Harvey continued. "Let me get you some coffee, I could do with one myself."

He sent a young duty officer to fetch the coffee.

"Les, the mayor would be happy to wipe the slate clean for you. No past criminal convictions to burden you. You seem like a good guy who deserves a break. What do you say to a fresh start? Hey, you could take off, do some travelling."

Harvey gave the gullible guy time to digest what had been said.

"Ok, what you wanna know then?"

"Anything you care to tell, buddy. You can start at the beginning, take your time, no rush."

"Well, I guess it started with a call from a guy I knew in jail. He knew I was in New York and wanted an errand done; 'nothing bad,' he told me, 'just deliver some cash to a client, get a signature for it, and fifty bucks is yours.' Well, I couldn't refuse an old ex-con, and fifty bucks would sure keep me going. I delivered a wad of notes, about $2,000 to a guy in a bar, and got him to sign something. Easiest fifty bucks I ever earned.

"'Don't even think of double-crossing me,' I was warned, ''cos I, and now you, work for Barclay. Remember him from prison?' he asked me."

"Good, Les, you're doing just fine. Here's the coffee. Officer, get this gent a snack."

Les continued to spill the beans as if relieved to be free from pressure.

"Tough guy was Barclay, could break your arm with his bare hand without him feeling a thing, detective. I sure remembered Barclay, everyone gave him a wide berth, gave him respect."

"Tell me, Les, do you remember names of any of the folk you delivered cash to? Or any information at all?"

Les thought hard. "Yeah, there was this lady, sad lady, drunk out of her mind – most of them were – signed the paperwork, almost kissed me; I backed off smart like. She stank of stale beer."

"You remember her name?"

Harvey's approach had the desired effect on the naïve man.

"Yeah, Clare something, no, Clara, that's it, lived not far from me, had a kid in juvie."

Harvey forced himself to keep calm. Here was the breakthrough they needed. Maybe this guy knew more.

"Good stuff, Les. The mayor's sure gonna thank you. Now, any other names you remember?"

"A guy from Chicago, got to know him real well, George North, gave him a bundle of dollars, 2,000. He was in a bar in downtown New York, said he needed the cash for computer stuff. There were loads of others: Stu Collins, Alan Campbell, Dale Greer—"

Harvey interrupted. "Tell me about Dale Greer."

"Not much to say, just another lowlife down on his

luck, something to do with bank troubles, went on about his wife and kids. I only met him once."

"You say you got to know George North. How come? Did you deliver more money?"

"No sir. Hey! I hope I get protection for this, can't risk big Barclay finding out I've been telling you guys this stuff."

"Don't worry, son, we'll protect you. Now, you were saying about George North…"

Harvey kept calm, hoping for a major breakthrough from the gullible man. Maybe this guy could help bring the crime to a swift conclusion and lead them to Lucy Mears.

"Yeah. Well, Alf, that's my ex-con buddy, he got me a job flying a private plane for some rich person. I had to pick up George North from airports, different ones each time, and fly him on to an isolated airfield where he was picked up by car. I had to wait for instructions to fly him back. Sometimes, it was days later."

"Oh yes, I see from the files here you were a pilot."

"Yeah, damned fine one too. Got caught pinching a few bottles of booze from the airline… everyone did it… I got jailed."

Harvey didn't expand on this. He knew the accused had been jailed for being drunk on the job and that drugs were found in his flight bag.

"Les, you've no idea how much nearer we are to finding that kid thanks to you. Tell me, where exactly did you fly George North to?"

Les, fired now with praise and enjoying being the centre of attention, told Harvey all he could recall about his flying assignments: the location and the airfields where he landed and took off from.

"Man, you should have seen the plane, pure luxury, a Gulfstream G150, great safety record…"

He continued to recite the dimensions, fuel consumption data, relating every small detail of the plane, his great love for flying clearly in evidence.

"Les, I think we could cut a deal here. I'll call the mayor and tell him what an ace guy you are. There's something we'd like you to do…"

Harvey briefed the buoyant Les as to what he was to do with regards to help locate the abductors of young Lucy.

"Top secret stuff, Les. Just between us, and think of the reward and your future life! Keep this number handy for anything you hear. I'm sure, like the rest of us, you want this poor kid found and returned to her rich mom. Hey, before you go, here's a ticket for a parking violation, not a real one, you understand. It's in case your buddies want to know why you were here in the precinct."

Les Soubry left the precinct dreaming of wealth and travel. *Might get me my own plane if the rich mom is grateful enough.*

CHAPTER 24

Harvey called his superintendent's office to ask for a rendezvous, as soon as possible.

"Can't you just tell me on the damn phone, man? I'm busy. Can't you schedule this for a less cluttered time?"

The superintendent was a brusque man who liked to run things his way.

"It's a sensitive issue, sir, one I need to discuss with you in total privacy. It's concerning disturbing news of the Mears kid."

"Ok, meet me here in an hour and make it brief. I have a lunch function to attend with the mayor and he hates being kept late."

Superintendent Benson slammed the phone down on Harvey.

"You might want to postpone lunch when you hear what I have to say, sir." Harvey spoke to a dead line.

He called Carr's office to update her on events.

"I'll go alone," he said, "to keep this among as few people as possible."

Superintendent Benson was visibly shaken on hearing what Harvey had to say.

"Good God, man, this is too much. Who else knows?"

"Only myself and Carole Carr, sir, she was with me when we questioned Brenda Mears. Detective Carr is the most discreet person I know."

"Bloody well better be. Make sure she keeps her mouth shut because this could ruin the guy."

Harvey thought how locating young Lucy seemed to have been dismissed by his boss at the stroke of a pen now that there was a more pressing mess to solve.

Superintendent Benson took the mayor aside. Mayor Carson was a burly man, more used to bullying than being bullied. His bulbous nose and rotund appearance told of a life of regular lavish civic lunches where alcohol was consumed in abundance and rich food in plentiful supply.

"I have alarming news to give you, sir. Can you spare me five?"

"As soon as this wretched lunch is over meet me in the library."

The mayor heard the news with unbelievable shock.

"This is preposterous and has to be concealed, it can't be made public. Who do you trust with this?"

"Harvey and Carr are trustworthy, sir, they won't breathe a word."

"Get them over here now."

The two arrived promptly, listening and nodding in agreement, as details were hammered out between their two superiors.

"No need to remind either of you of the gravity of this assignment, complete silence on it, not a word to your families or colleagues. We don't want any bigmouth talking in the pub or any pillow talk. Explain your absence only to your family, tell them it is a routine task and you will be away a few nights, hopefully less. The department is being hammered financially with this case. Wrap it up as quickly as possible, find the guy, ask the questions and get the hell back here."

"Yes, Mayor, we fully understand the implications of it—"

"As for your colleagues," cut in Superintendent Benson, "assign them a task to keep them well occupied and away from the office, so that there's no attempt to contact you two for several days. Keep them busy."

***

Back at base, Harvey's squad were each assigned a task that he hoped would keep them occupied for many hours, days even, and make them unaware of his and Carr's absence. Once the squad had departed to their various tasks, the two waited until the coast was clear, collected their belongings and drove in Carr's sedan to Chicago O'Hare to catch a flight to Washington D.C. As they pulled away from the precinct, Kip O'Rourke, suspicious that his bosses had said nothing of their own duties for the forthcoming days, had held back, unseen, to observe their move.

Carr's sedan? Now that's unusual for them not to use a squad car, what's going on here then?

He promptly called his mate.

"Something's going on here, Sonny. Carr's heading out with the boss in her sedan, heading north. Can you pick up a trace? They never use personal vehicles for police work."

"I'm on to it, trust Sonny on this! Keep your phone free. I've already picked up something suspicious from Harvey's trace. He called Superintendent Benson who sounded panic stricken and said he had to call the mayor."

Kip thought, *What are these guys up to, calling the super and the mayor and keeping it quiet?*

Sonny wished he had bugged Harvey's jacket. He caught snippets of crackling conversation as the sedan headed towards O'Hare. *I should have invested in better*

129

stuff. Sonny gasped when he picked up what they were talking about… *Holy shit, this is big!*

"Kip, they're heading to O'Hare. I'm gonna follow them. My snooper was right about what we discussed. Oh man, this is gonna blow things apart!"

He spotted them at the check-in desk for Washington D.C. and called his editor for permission to fly to D.C.

"You think this newspaper has a bottomless pit for you to go on endless road trips? Remember the last one, Vegas? You were dead cert you'd found a lead on the Sharkey murder. Remember? Total crap, Sonny, and cost us dear!"

"Trust me on this one, boss, it's big… it's a lead on the missing Mears kid."

"Better be good then, Sonny, or there's no job for you to come back to. I want receipts for all your expenses."

Sonny purchased his ticket to Washington D.C. and called his buddy Kip to fill him in on what he had heard.

"Say that again? You saying he definitely is the father of that kid? Man, this will ruin him."

"Listen up, Kip, this is what I need you to do…"

Kip O'Rourke listened to instructions from his buddy.

"Got it, Sonny. I'll keep this line open and let you know the minute I hear any more buzz from here at the precinct. Same goes for you, keep the info coming."

CHAPTER 25

The travellers, weary and physically exhausted, stopped often to sleep. Lucy was again given a mild sedation to help relieve her of the tediousness of the relentless expedition. They were well behind the schedule set for them.

***

The buoyant politician answered questions fired at him with the skill of a master orator. A reporter, sidling nearer the podium, caught his eye and prepared to fire his query. Ross smiled innocently, ready for the guy's question.

"Sir, tell us about your family. How do they feel about the prospect of perhaps living in the White House?"

Ross laughed. "The boys are as excited as Linda-Mae and me. Plenty of room for growing kids to run around."

The reporter hadn't finished. "Sir," he continued, "and your daughter? Will she move there with you?"

"You misunderstand," he replied. "I have two sons, Jake and Ben, great kids, a credit to their mom here."

He hugged his beaming wife in affirmation. As he was about to take another question, the reporter, not to be easily dismissed, asked, "Sir, with respect, I refer to your fifteen-year-old daughter, Lucy Mears, heiress to the Mears Empire of Chicago. Where is she, sir? Have you hidden her away? She's been missing for ten weeks now."

The hall fell silent, gasps were heard. Ross S.

Witherspoon looked stunned, his face ashen. Slowly, very slowly, the agonizing truth dawned on him. He looked at the bemused faces of his supporters who willed him to make things right for them.

"Hell, no!" Steve Wilkes reacted quickly, guided his prodigy by the arm and commanded, "Get the hell out of here, use the back door."

He led the numb man and his startled wife towards the rear of the building. Uproar descended in the venue as the implication of the disclosure hit home. The abduction of Lucy Mears was well documented. Very few people in that auditorium would not have heard of her. Suddenly, an event that began hundreds of miles from their cosseted lives took on a momentous sense of urgency. Voices rose from the incredulous crowd. Volume increased as disbelief turned to bewilderment. People turned to each other, questions flying around the room as the faithful supporters tried to make sense of events.

The reporter who instigated the chaos was nowhere to be seen. He had discarded his jacket, donned a "Vote for Ross" sweater and mingled unnoticed in the mayhem, secretly recording the uproar, which went directly to his editor.

"Good man, Sonny," the editor whispered to him as the special edition was published online.

Linda-Mae Witherspoon dissolved in tears at her husband's faltering confession.

"I was young, honey, a juvenile fling, so long ago. It didn't mean a thing. I never knew about the kid. That bitch told me she'd got rid of it. She tricked me. I even gave her money for an abortion. Oh, hell, this will ruin me, my future's gone up in smoke."

"Your future?" screamed the distressed wife. "What about my future, what about the kids? I've given everything to you: time, money, unflinching support. You have shamed us, Ross."

Steve Wilkes, coming between the warring couple, looked directly at his client.

"Ross, you assured me you were squeaky clean and I believed you; nevertheless and thankfully, I had my guys check you out. This only came to my attention an hour ago and it's too big to handle. Lucy Mears! The kid's been on every website, newspaper and TV channel for weeks. Every voter in the country knows of her. I have to ask you, man, do you know anything of her abduction and whereabouts?"

"Good heavens, Steve! I didn't know of her existence until ten minutes ago. I've been too busy to watch TV or read anything online or in newspapers other than poll ratings. You have to believe me."

At the Witherspoon home, Linda-Mae's parents were transfixed to their TV, glad they had sent the boys to the den to play with their latest gizmo. Visibly shaken, they were at first sceptical at the confusion, furious with the reporter for spreading bullshit, then concerned for their daughter as the truth dawned and they realized their son-in-law had not denied the allegation thrown at him.

"If this is true, he's finished politically, isn't he?" asked Betty Sheringham of her stunned husband.

"Truth is, honey, he is finished now. Hope to hell he's not involved in that poor kid's disappearance. We need to be strong for Linda-Mae and the boys. The backlash of this will be horrific."

The backlash was indeed horrific, reverberating through the country. The presidential campaign, now in tatters, came to an abrupt standstill.

***

In Chicago, Myra Hill was in her office at Mears Empire with her TV on in the background as she worked at her desk while occasionally following her favoured candidate's campaign. She ran screaming to her boss's office, calling for her to come immediately. Brenda, hoping against hope for news of her daughter, rushed in expectantly, only to be caught in an unimaginable maelstrom.

"This is outrageous!" she cried. "How dare they bring my child into this? Who the hell released this information?"

Her team, alerted by the shouting, rushed to Myra's office and looked on bemused, knowing nothing of Brenda's past affairs and never ever questioning Lucy's parentage.

"I should have confided in you guys before now. I guess I wanted to wait until Lucy was old enough to understand. I indeed dated Ross Witherspoon for many months. He dumped me, told me to get rid of the baby, threw some money at me and never entered my life again, that is, until now. He honestly knew nothing of Lucy's existence. Who? Who has disclosed this?"

"Oh honey," comforted Justin, hugging the weeping woman. "We're all here for you, always will be."

**

Harvey and Carr arrived in Washington D.C. and planned to stay out of sight while President-elect Witherspoon finished his speech and had taken some questions. They aimed to speak to him at the end of the session. They arrived at the venue as furore erupted.

"What's going on?" asked Harvey as they struggled to enter the building where people were stampeding out, each clutching a phone to their ear as, one by one, the incredulous supporters related their own versions of events to the world.

The detectives made their way to the rear of the building in time to see the shamed public official and his wife escorted to a car, which took off at high speed. Harvey's phone rang. Superintendent Benson hollered down the line at him, "Who the hell was that reporter? Who told him about this?"

Harvey had no reply for his irate boss.

"Get your butts back here as soon as and report directly to me; you'd better have some good answers for me."

Unable to make contact with Ross S. Witherspoon or his staff, they returned to Dulles. On the flight back to Chicago, Harvey and Carr caught up with news of the Washington fiasco from the web. They knew no more than that which had been reported in the media.

Over the next few days the political world was in turmoil. A new candidate would have to be found. Time was of the essence and voters' trust had to be restored. No mean feat!

The Witherspoons did not return to their home. Instead, they were driven to the Sheringham's lakeside retreat, where they hoped they would have time to calm down and assess their situation. No one looked forward to the reunion. When the horrendous news broke, the grandparents promptly gathered things together and, with the boys in the car, headed for their lakeside home, the boys excited at the prospect of an unexpected holiday.

"What about school, Grandpa?"

"That can wait for now, Ben."

***

As Steve Wilkes continued his instructions to the couple, Ross S. Witherspoon sat with his head in his hands, bemoaning his past dalliance, his political future in shreds.

"Don't use your mobile phones till we check, could be bugged, my guys are working on it. Who let this story out?"

"It's over," mumbled the disgraced man.

✽✽✽

Once Brenda had calmed down sufficiently, she called Molly, saying she was heading home. By the time she reached her Lincoln Park home she had to run the gauntlet of reporters, TV crews and sightseers.

"Any truth in what's been said, Ms. Mears?"

"Where's your daughter then, have you hidden her away with her father?"

"Are you in collusion with Witherspoon?"

Hurtful questions assailed her ears as she fought her way to her home.

"Close the shades, Nora," she instructed as she rushed indoors. "Make sure all doors are secure, we don't want peepers."

"We did that when we got the first whiff of reporters, but the landline has not stopped ringing," sobbed Molly.

"We can't leave it off. Lucy might try to get in touch. I take it you both saw the fiasco in Washington?"

"We did. Can we reassure you, neither of us revealed any information at any time to anyone," continued Molly.

"Molly, Nora, with all my heart I believe you. My gut tells me one or other of those detectives spilt the beans, probably for cash. Meanwhile, we keep our heads down. Don't leave the house, either of you."

✽✽✽

Benson, fuming with rage, steam almost emitting from the top of his balding head, interrogated the detectives, blaming them fully for breaking the sensitive information to the unknown reporter. He was unwilling to give them any slack.

"The mayor is incensed at this mess, on at me every hour to sort it out, wants my head on a plate. I'll sort it out, damned sure I will. How much were you guys paid? Heck, I thought you were my most trusted colleagues. You're both suspended, as from now. Hand in your badges on the way out. Stick around your homes for further questioning. I haven't finished with either of you!"

"Sir," Carr attempted to protest. "Sir, we did not do this. You are accusing us unfairly."

"Unfair!" screeched Benson. "The future of the presidency is in jeopardy because of you assholes."

"Sir, we are not to blame. You're way out wrong on this," Harvey protested, his face red with rage.

"Suspended. Now get out, this interview is over."

The aggrieved detectives had no option but to leave Benson's office.

As they made their way along the corridor, Kip O'Rourke, who had an eldritch knack of appearing where least wanted, came out of his office and in all innocence spoke to his superior officers.

"Hey, you guys. You ok? Thought I heard raised voices from the boss's office, anything I can do?"

Harvey growled at the loathsome man, "Yeah, get out of our way."

Benson sent for O'Rourke.

"Officer O'Rourke, you are temporarily promoted. I'm putting you in charge of the Mears case. Get this fiasco solved, as soon as. Use whatever resources you have at your disposal. We've been let down by two trustworthy officers, Harvey and Carr. Their treachery has shocked me to the core. You think you know people – just goes to show, Kip lad. Burn the candle at both ends."

"Yes, sir, we are all hurting at their double-dealing, but you can rely on me. I'll solve this mess."

"Good, man, good, now get going."

An elated Kip O'Rourke settled himself in Harvey's office, re-arranged the room to suit, and gloated.

"Well, Carole Carr, got yah!"

Still sneering, he summoned his team but nor before pouring himself a congratulatory drink from Harvey's desk drawer.

"Cheers, Kip boy!"

CHAPTER 26

The Chief of Bureau of Detectives, Tony Harvey, sat at home, shocked at his unjust treatment, determined to find the informant who wreaked havoc on the coming elections, on himself and Carr, and on the search for Lucy Mears. Carole Carr, equally confounded and angry, changed into her leisure wear and went for a long walk with Walt, her trusted mutt.

"Come on, Walt, you're the only one with any sense. Let's go for a hike to clear my head of this mess."

As Carole jogged along with Walt, her feisty mutt, his boundless energy never failed to amaze her.

"Hey, Walt, wait for me!"

Walt had been with the family for eleven years. Despite his age, he frolicked like the puppy he still believed himself to be and seldom left Carole's side when she was at home, preferring her company to that of the boisterous kids who shared his life. She fumed over the events leading to her and her colleagues suspension. *How did that reporter find out about Witherspoon? Who leaked the story? Surely not the mayor? The superintendent? I doubt it. They were dumbfounded with the news. Can't be either of them, surely. Who the hell did it? As soon as the kids are in bed and Ted's gone to choir practice I'll call Tony and see if he can make sense of events.*

Carole continued her jog, prevented Walt from wandering too far, and returned home to shower and change.

"Ok, kids, let's have a story before bedtime!"

Her lively kids settled down to hear *Freddie's Friday Freckles*, yet again. Later that evening, she called Tony Harvey. A rather inebriated Tony attempted to talk sense. Carole led the one-sided conversation and arranged to call round the next day to discuss the matter.

"I can see how you're coping!" she laughed as she finished the call.

Next day, the pair sat in his bachelor pad, deep in conversation as they attempted to identify the snitch.

"Who, apart from us, knew about Witherspoon; well, other than the super and the mayor? Who would benefit from giving information to a reporter?" Tony continued. "If we were at work, I'd call in that damn reporter and kick ass till I got results."

"Me too," responded Carole. "We may have to do some undercover work ourselves. I'm not for sitting around watching my career flounder. Are you up for a bit of cloak and dagger stuff? Let's see what we can dig up from that newspaper. We can hang out in that bar frequented by the media guys. You never know what we might find out."

"Yeah, let's go. We'll take your car, ok? Mine needs some attention, never seem to have time to see to it."

"Tony, you've never had that car checked over in all the time I've known you."

Outside, she dropped her keys. Tony, always the gentleman, stooped to retrieve them from under the sedan. He stood up, made a "keep quiet" gesture with his finger on his lips and moved his colleague out of range of the vehicle, took her arm and walked her to the safety of a nearby coffee shop.

"Your car's been bugged. Maybe, just maybe, we're on

to our squealer. We keep this to ourselves; don't know about you, but right now, I don't trust too many of our co-workers. Is there a weak link in our squad?"

"Could well be. We'd best check our homes. I hate to think that anyone has invaded my privacy and listened to Ted and me and the kids."

They abandoned the idea of visiting the bar and went back to retrieve the car. Aware that their voices could be monitored, they drove home in silence. Carole turned the music on at full volume.

"You need to clean this condo. It looks like you've been burgled. You live like this, Tony?"

"Never have time for chores."

"You have plenty of time now. Get to it!"

They found nothing suspicious at either of their homes.

"Here's the plan, Carole. We drive your sedan with the device still activated until it's out of range, then I can have a look at it."

Carole drove the sedan some distance with Tony lying on the floor to avoid detection. When they were sure the bug could no longer detect their position, the car came to a halt.

"Hell, do you always drive like a maniac? Every bone in my body is mashed."

He carefully retrieved the device and studied it.

"Right then. This is a GSM bug. It can be placed in a vehicle or room, transmits like a mobile phone bug anywhere mobile network exists. They are known as infinity bugs and can be linked to other devices, other similar bugs. Where we are right now there's no signal, so I can dismantle it carefully."

"So you say this device here can be linked to another?"

"Yeah, as long as they are in range. As I say, we are ok

out here, mobile signal is almost non-existent. It's a good quality wire-tap, but whoever set it up set it for short range. We've checked our homes, so probably this is the only one… or maybe not. What about our offices?"

"Hell, yes, there could be one of those links there. We need to get into that building, Tony. Could be anywhere, but my guess is one or other of our offices."

"And just how do you plan to do that, ma'am? Just walk in and say, 'hey guys, I'm in search of bugging devices'?"

"Is that gizmo thing still active?"

"It will be when it's in range… not at the moment obviously."

"Can we use it to connect to the source?"

"Umm, leave it with me. I'll research this."

"Be careful, Tony, we don't know who we're dealing with."

"Not yet, Carole, not yet."

***

Kip O'Rourke sat in Harvey's office, unaware of the bug planted there by his friend Sonny. Tony Harvey entered the room, much to O'Rourke's shock.

"Hey, Tony, how's it going? You supposed to be here?"

"Left my phone here when I left in a hurry, have you come across it, Kip?" he said as he rummaged in the desk drawer.

"Hey, you can't do that…"

Harvey lifted an almost empty bottle of Scotch from a drawer.

"Well, I'll be damned, was sure I had more in that bottle. Hey, I'll have to watch my drinking."

Kip reddened, knowing he'd been rumbled. Harvey, however, more concerned with other matters, said no more.

"You shouldn't be here. I'm going for the super."

Kip O'Rourke raced out to find his boss. Harvey quickly located a small insipid device, made an adjustment, and replaced it before heading for the exit. He spotted O'Rourke, held up his mobile phone and hollered, "Got it, Kip! I'll be out of your face."

In Carr's smart kitchen, the two waited tentatively for action from the device removed from the sedan to the kitchen and linked to the one in O'Rourke's office. Harvey, impatient for a result, rhythmically tapped the table, irritating his colleague.

"Hell, Tony, stop that... be patient."

Several cups of coffee later, patience was rewarded when the device buzzed in to life, making Carole jump.

"Sonny," hollered a familiar voice. "Harvey's been back in the office; hell, what if he knows something?"

"Calm down, man, check if the bug's still in place under the second drawer, it should pulsate if it's still working."

Kip O'Rourke clumsily located the device.

"Affirmative, it's here and working fine. You should have told me you'd planted it here; how did you get into the building?"

"That's for me to know and you to find out!" chortled the reporter.

"What about the one in her sedan? You told me about that one."

"I'll check it out, hold on. Crackling came through the gadget on Carr's table, startling her yet again, but not disturbing her demeanour.

"Yeah, buddy, it's ok, still in place, active, so no problem there. It's still in her car; I drove past her place earlier, car's parked in its usual place. Keep calm, Kip. My editor's giving me a big, I mean big, bonus and you'll get your share. Now get off this line, don't use it unless it's really important."

Clicks were heard. Harvey kept his finger over his lips to warn Carole to remain silent. After a few more minutes, they grinned at each other.

"Got them! Check that recording before we become euphoric!"

Carole operated a tiny recording device that Tony had rigged up and there, for all to hear, was the conversation they had just heard.

"Got you, you assholes! Let's go find Superintendent Benson."

Benson, with detectives Harvey and Carr in tow, walked in to Kip's office. On seeing them, the bent officer paled significantly, knowing that something daunting was about to happen. "Kip James O'Rourke. I'm placing you under arrest. Detective Carr, read him his Miranda."

"My pleasure, sir."

Simultaneously in a local newspaper office, FBI agents entered the building, arrested the editor and reporter Sonny Woods, sent staff home and closed the organization down.

"Go find other jobs," one agent told them. "This joint won't open for the longest time."

Media channels reported that police had arrested three people in connection with the toppling of presidential candidate Ross S. Witherspoon, whose whereabouts were unknown.

That evening, Harvey joined Carole and her husband, Ted, for a celebratory meal at Carr's home.

"Uncle Tony! Uncle Tony," screamed two excitable kids. "Do some magic tricks for us."

Tony kept the kids amused while Carole attended to the meal and Ted to the drinks.

"Tony," she laughed. "You need to get yourself a good woman, settle down and have some kids!"

"What! And have them upset my apple pie condo?"

Harvey excused himself to take an incoming call, then came back into the room with good news for his colleague.

"The lab have discovered that the vial containing the sedative that Clara Blake handed in came from a hospital in Chicago where a nurse, Rita Hampton, was dismissed for stealing drugs. Our guys are on to tracking her down. According to a neighbour, she moved to New York to nurse a relative. They were able to trace the vial from the batch number."

"New York seems to be where we have to concentrate our search for Lucy," Carr remarked.

"The mystery deepens though," continued Harvey. "A garage owner in Wisconsin reported a possible link to the kid. Some of our colleagues there are interviewing the guy, it may be nothing…"

CHAPTER 27

Fate had led Zelda and Kristof to a new, somewhat terrifying stage in their lives. They arrived with some trepidation at the address given by Rita.

"We're taking a risk coming here, Kristof; we don't know what we're facing."

"It's a risk we have to take, dragi. We must try to secure a better future. I trust our new acquaintance. I'm sure she's sincere. We can always leave if the employment doesn't suit us."

When Kristof pulled the doorbell, they were admitted to a palatial house, the likes of which they had never seen before, except in films. Rita welcomed them warmly, sensed their fear and anxiety and reassured them that all would be well. Zelda was in awe of her new surroundings.

"Boss is waiting to meet you. That is how you will address your employer at all times, 'Boss'. Come with me."

Rita led them through the house to a room on another floor where they met Boss for the first time.

"Tell me your story in your own words. Rita has given me some details of your plight, but I'd sure like to hear it from your own lips. Boss settled in a high-backed leather chair while Kristof related events. He told of the siege of Sarajevo; the loss of family; Zelda's miscarriage; their journey through Europe; the befriending of Donata and Marc; and their arrival in New York. He told of how luck led him to meet Rita and how his wish to seek employment led him here.

Boss listened without interruption. When Kristof, holding his wife's hand, had finished relating their sad tale, Boss sat quietly making unnerving eye contact with the two, before commenting.

"That's some story! I'm sure impressed by your honesty in returning Rita's purse when you could have used the money for yourselves."

"Zelda and I could never be anything but honest, in spite of our hardships. True, that money could have helped us, but we could never take what wasn't ours."

Zelda, who had been quiet throughout, overawed at the exquisite décor and her husband's eloquence, nodded in agreement as he spoke.

Boss continued. "Yeah, I can see that. Your openness has impressed me. I would like you to work for me in whatever capacity I require. There's good accommodation here in an apartment above the garage in the grounds. It's small, but adequate for two people. Rita will show you around the estate and help you settle in while you familiarize yourselves with the house and gardens."

Over the next few months the two settled to a new routine: Kristof helped outdoors in the vast gardens and greenhouses, while Zelda's duties were mainly household chores. The hours were long and the work rewarding. They both became more robust and healthier as the weeks went on.

"Have you noticed how ill Boss looks?" asked Zelda of her husband on the rare occasion they found time to enjoy their little apartment. Her nursing skills had detected a gaunt, sickly look in her employer.

"I saw some medication when I was cleaning Boss's room; I'm sure they are cancer drugs."

After some months in their new surroundings, Boss sent for the couple and without preamble spoke out.

"I have had someone look into your backgrounds. I keep a strict check on all my employees. I don't think you have been upfront with me, have you? Have you stonewalled me?"

Kristof looked bemused; Zelda tried to assimilate where Boss was leading.

"Kristof, Zelda," Boss addressed them, "or should I say Nikol and Amila Tanovic? You have no visas to be here, have you? No official permission?"

Kristof became fearful and the colour drained from his face.

"Please, please don't have us deported. We came to this country with only good intentions to start a new life and work hard. We can't go back to the hell we left."

Boss studied the anxious faces of the new employees. Zelda sobbed quietly.

"As long as you remain loyal to me and follow my instructions to the letter, then you will be perfectly safe. Betray me in any way and things will be very different."

"We have no choice, Boss, we are grateful and owe you. You can rely on us both," replied Kristof, his heart pounding in his chest so much so he thought he might go into cardiac arrest. He detected a harshness in Boss never perceived before; a fear came over him, a fear he had not felt for many months, a fear that he had forgotten existed. Zelda sat in stony silence, thinking their world was about to crumble.

Boss continued. "I have a special assignment for you, it's essential you follow it exactly. A lot is riding on this being carried out without any changes being made by you to my plan.

They sat in silence, listening intently to what was being asked of them, alarm and dread filling their hearts, but they knew there was no alternative for them, save deportation. The assignment involved collecting a child, and keeping her sedated and safe. They were to drive some thousands of miles by a convoluted route mapped out for them, with no deviation to be taken, and make calls to Boss on specific dates. They were to cross many states, involving several weeks of travel and rest, to a cabin in Montana where they were to remain with their young charge until summoned to return, retracing their steps as instructed. They packed personal items and prepared for the strangest of tasks.

"Crazy," muttered Kristof, "to drive continually, thousands of miles, just to return again! At least we can share the driving."

"But we must do it, we can't afford not to. To disobey would be disastrous for us. Boss said all would be revealed to us on our return."

"What's it all in aid of? So mysterious, so strangely odd," said Kristof, as he turned over to attempt to sleep before venturing on an epic journey.

CHAPTER 28

The cabin in Montana at Yellow Bay State Park was off the beaten track and difficult to reach, the terrain putting strain on the overworked campervan, resulting in disaster when a tyre burst, leaving them stranded in deep snow. Kristof jumped down to investigate.

"This can't be fixed in this weather; the blizzard's fierce and light is fading fast. We will have to continue on foot as best we can."

"How far are we from the cabin?"

"Difficult to tell in these conditions, but I don't think it's far, we will just have to walk."

"Oh, no!" wailed Zelda, knowing there was no option but to trek the last stretch to safety.

Wrapped up well, the trio struggled uphill, Kristof making a path for the others to walk in his footsteps, the frightened child clinging to Zelda, putting her whole weight on her, which made the slog even more arduous. Kristof carried a backpack crammed with as much as he could carry, his steps slow and wearisome, as he led the jaded group on through the fierce storm. The path, as far as he could ascertain, veered towards a clearing where stood a welcoming sight.

"The cabin!" Kristof pointed, his tense muscles visibly relaxing.

The cabin itself was comfortably set out and heated up quickly. An abundant store of dried foodstuff filled the cupboard as well as some homemade pies, which delighted the hungry travellers. As Kristof unpacked the backpack, distributing the items, hoping he had not left anything essential behind, Zelda rustled up a quick meal, after which she settled Lucy to sleep before she and her exhausted husband relaxed by the log fire with a welcome drink.

"This is some place. Everything we need is here; someone must come and replenish food and gather logs. It's all very intriguing," mumbled a weary Zelda.

Next day, Kristof had to call Boss. The signal from the cabin was intermittent due to weather conditions, so he had no option but to retrace his steps to the troublesome campervan to tackle the problem tyre as best he could. He carefully drove the seventeen miles or so to Polson in the hope of making the call and having the badly damaged tyre replaced. The journey was treacherous; the road was covered in ice, no highway personnel would venture out there to deal with a burst tyre, even if Boss had allowed it. Progress was slow; the damaged tyre made the journey even more dangerous, heavy snow blinded his eyes and caused him unimaginable stress as he struggled at times to keep the vehicle from slipping off the path.

Zelda and Lucy played board games, which they found in the cabin. Lucy, now aware that she had no control over her situation, had bonded with Zelda and sensed in her a warm human being who, for reasons unknown to her, could not divulge details of their marathon journey. Zelda reassured her as best she could that no harm would come to her and soon she would be told everything. "I just want to go home, Zelda. Can't you call Mama? She must be frantic… are you holding me to ransom? My mother will pay what you ask, please call Mama."

"If only I could, my dear, if only… we are under strict

instructions and cannot deviate from them or we three could be in danger. I cannot tell you anything else, not yet."

"You're afraid of someone, aren't you?"

In spite of her young age, Lucy had sensed fear.

"Who are you afraid of?"

"Hush, child!" scolded her minder, mad at herself for showing her emotion.

"No more questions."

The exhausted man returned to the cabin, his ordeal over. Taking his wife aside out of earshot of Lucy, he related the latest instructions from Boss.

"The forecast seems to predict an improvement soon. We have to stay here some days more and return to base, taking as many days as it took to get here."

"What an ordeal for the child," said Zelda. "If we feel strained, how much worse is it for her? She's such a sweet child, I feel so bad about all this."

"We have no option, dragi, we have to see it through and soon we shall be free."

"Will we ever be truly free?" sighed Zelda.

**

Lucy woke early to the winter sun shining through the little window of her room; the snow had stopped, there was a definite thaw. Water plopped from the roof, making rhythmic sounds as it fell to the gravel path beneath her window. The view took her breath away, the sun sending sparkles of light on to Flathead Lake, causing her to reflect on the beauty of the place. *This is so amazing*, she thought.

She felt a peace she had not experienced since her captivity touching her heart as she studied the scene before her.

Zelda and Kristof were still asleep in an adjoining room. Zelda had told her to have some cookies should she feel hungry. She made her way quietly to the kitchen, stopping to admire the changing vista from different windows in the snug cabin. *Glorious scenery!* she thought as she sat munching on a cookie, pondering on who owned such a winsome property and why she was there. She sighed and made to return to her room when she spotted Kristof's mobile phone. In a nanosecond, she grasped it. *I'm going to call Mama.* She had overheard Kristof mention that the signal was unreliable due to the storm, but took her chance on there being some reception now that the weather was calmer. In her excitement Lucy punched in the only number she could remember. It was a private number that took her directly to her mother's phone and was elated to hear it ring and be picked up immediately.

"Mother!" she cried. "Mother, get me home. Why are you doing this to me?"

Zelda gently removed the phone from the trembling girl's hand and switched it off, saying, "Not yet, honey, not yet."

Lucy ran to her room, threw her quaking body onto the bed and wept sorely. She was so distraught she did not hear the couple's raised voices as Zelda berated her husband for his carelessness.

"We can't afford to make mistakes like that. Keep your phone with you at all times."

***

Brenda, ecstatic at hearing her daughter's voice, ran through the house shouting for Molly.

"Lucy called me! She called me!"

Molly hugged the shocked woman, listened to her garbled version of the brief call and cried with her friend.

"We know she's alive then, but where is she?"

"We were cut off, it was a bad signal."

"Get hold of Detective Harvey, tell him what's happened."

Brenda sobbed. "It was strange, Molly, she asked me why I was doing this to her. What does she mean? Call Myra at the office, give her the news."

Brenda threw herself into Molly's arms; it was as if the stresses of the past weeks had restored Brenda's sense of decency.

Attempts to contact the detective proved difficult; no one seemed to know where the guy was. His mobile phone went unanswered, as did that of his teammate Carr. The two detectives were attending a court hearing regarding the recent events in Washington and were unable to be contacted.

"Where are these people when we need them?" cried Brenda in frustration.

Nora, alerted by the screams, joined her mother and Brenda.

The junior officer on desk duty was unsure how he should proceed when all attempts to contact his immediate superior failed. He felt the matter required urgent action and made the decision to call further up the chain to Superintendent Benson. *I might as well be hung for a sheep as a lamb*, he thought as he punched in the direct number taking him straight to Superintendent Benson.

"It's concerning the missing Mears girl, sir."

***

Superintendent Benson presented himself at Brenda's home and apologized for Harvey's and Carr's absence, stating they were out of town on essential departmental business. He declined to state the specific nature of their duty, thinking perhaps Brenda had more than enough to cope with. He brought a technician with him to examine the phone.

"Wilson here will attempt to retrieve the last number."

As they waited for a result, the officer's fingers worked expertly across the keys. Benson gently obtained from the tearful mother details of her daughter's call.

"It was so brief. It lasted seconds before I heard a click as if someone had switched it off."

Wilson shook his head. "Sorry, sir, the number can't be retrieved; the call wasn't long enough for me to trace. I would need to take it to the lab to test it further."

"I can't be without it, that's my private number that Lucy might call back on," lamented Brenda.

"Ok, we'll bring some more equipment here and attempt to find the data. At least we know she's alive. Hold on to that," said Benson as he left to return to base to contact Harvey.

Dejection filled the household; the moment of elation had passed.

CHAPTER 29

Lucy continued to sob and stare out of the window of the little room in the cabin, deep in private thought.

How did it get to this? Why couldn't my mother be more like Gina? I love sleepovers with Abigail. Gina's a cool mom. She's lively, funny and so loving. Her eyes light up with laughter, like sparkles. She's so pretty! Her flawless skin and her hair glow like the sun dancing across them, just like Abigail's. Gina, Abbie, I miss you!

Lucy wiped her tears and continued her monologue and reminiscing.

Gina, I would say, "I love your floral arrangements, you are so creative!"

"Thanks, Lucy, that's sweet, but you know, you're just as creative, if not more so, but in a different way. Your music is so special, honey, you have talent. We'll see you in the Chicago Symphony Orchestra someday, of that I'm sure!"

"That's my aim, Gina, to join CSO as the best cellist ever and travel the world with them. Ken says I can take my dream to the ends of the earth."

"He's darn right, honey. Aim high."

"But my mother... Gina, you know her. You know how she is. She wants me to study business management and follow her into Mears Empire. She thinks my music is a hobby... how can she not see I'm passionate about music and it's not part time? It is my life. I'd hate to be in business, I loathe the idea."

Lucy continued with her dreams as the snow gently tapped the little window of her cosy room, as if trying to soothe her spirit.

"Lucy," my mother would say. "Your great-grandfather started this business from nothing, built it on hard work, taught his son everything he needed to know to expand the firm and take it from strength to strength. He in turn passed his passion on to me, and look where we are: one of the top publishing businesses in Chicago, well respected and trusted. You have to carry on the family firm. It will be handed to you on a plate. Once you have graduated from Chicago Business School, then post grad at Cornell, you will have a place on the board and I'll teach you everything you need to know to take over from me someday."

"Mother!" I would reply. "I don't want that! You know I want to study music at North Western."

"Lucy, we will discuss this later. I have a meeting with the auditors in an hour."

That was as far as I ever got, trying to discuss my life with her. She was always busy, forever running to meetings, here and there, always on her phone. No wonder I turn to Mama, dear Molly. I've called her mama for as long as I can remember. I grew up thinking Molly was my mama and Nora, my elder sister. Mama nurtured me, was always there, and told me stories at bedtime.

I loved those tales of her beloved Ireland and the songs she sang. The less I saw of my mother, the more I saw of Molly and Nora... Oh, why am I in this place with these people?

Lucy, now lost in thoughts of home, continued to ponder.

Dear Molly, Mama, so tall and straight, facing the

world with a frankness that challenged anyone to defy her right to be the person she was. She was well built and when she chuckled, as she often did, her whole body shook.

"Do you miss Ireland, Mama?" I would say to her.

"Oh, mavourneen," she told me "It's a distant memory now. I left Donegal when I was a seven year old, never returned, although I always had a mind to. My folks came over here to make a better life for themselves."

"Would you ever go back and visit?"

"Not much point. I've no relatives there now apart from a distant cousin who's in assisted living in Dublin. I never met her, only heard of her through my mammy's talk of her side of the family. No, honey, my memories of the old country come from stories and songs that I learned from my folks."

As always, spending time in Mama's company calmed my mood. Mama hugged me as she asked,

"So, sweetie, what's caused the latest upset with your mother?"

"The usual, Mama. She won't listen when I want to discuss my future; she thinks my music is only a hobby. I'll soon have to decide on serious study subjects… she won't see past me going to CBS. I'm not going there, I'm definitely not! I would hate to be in business school."

Molly pursed her lips in anger, a trait I'd come to recognize over the years when she wanted to speak her mind, but loyalty forbade it.

"She'll come up with some nightmare plan for me, I know she will! She always gets her own way."

Molly sighed. She knew well how my mother's mind worked. From an early age, she had reared her. She told me my mother showed an independent spirit, a stubbornness, which helped her become a successful businessperson, but at what cost?

Lucy's memories came flooding back as she tried to make sense of her situation.

"Mama," I remember saying. "I'm growing up. You'd think she'd realize I have a future, one I want for myself."

"Sure, and don't I know it! Sixteen next birthday! Where has time gone? Seems no time at all since I came here with Nora and took charge of your mother, such a sweet babe... and then, you yourself, reared you like my own..."

Molly's voice trailed off as she lost herself in memories.

Catching her mood, I should have let things go, but stubbornness seems to be a trait in my family and I blurted out, "Mama, do you know who my father is?"

I'd never raised this subject with her before. I had interrupted her reverie. Molly, visibly shaken by the unexpected question, drew a deep intake of breath, turned away and sternly told me never to ask that question of her.

"So you do know, don't you? Please tell me. I have a right to know, haven't I? Who is he?"

"Yes, sweetie, you do have that right, but it's not for me to tell... you have to ask your mother."

"And you think she'll tell me?"

I almost roared in frustration. That was the first time I had ever shouted at dear mama. I took off to my music room where I found solace. Music soothed my soul.

CHAPTER 30

Molly, visibly upset at Lucy's question, threw herself into her baking, attacking the dough as if to release tension within her. Her body shook with anger, not at Lucy, but with the unfeeling Brenda. Her thoughts wandered to one occasion when she attempted to interfere in a mother/daughter dispute, only to be put down firmly by her boss.

"I'm her mother, Molly. I will make that decision."

Molly reddened as she recalled the rebuke. That moment was the turning point in her relationship when she relinquished any emotional responsibility and became simply an employee.

Suppose it had to come someday.

Molly well remembered the day she took up residence with the Mears and met baby Brenda for the first time.

Such a cutie, I thought, as Simon Mears placed the wriggling infant in my arms. We bonded quickly; Nora adored her kid "sister". As Simon's business expanded, he left more and more of the care to me, but he did make a point of being home for bedtime, but these visits became fewer and fewer and I found myself in total care of the child. Ours was a close relationship, which changed when she completed her post-grad degree and took her place with her father on the board of Mears Empire.

She had always confided in me about her various boyfriends; I consoled her when they parted, rejoiced when they filled her life with laughter and picked up the pieces when disaster struck. And it did.

Brenda became pregnant by the young politician she had been dating for many months, but the relationship wasn't to last.

I never saw her as mad as she was when he ended the relationship. Her poor father was at a loss to console her, but his headstrong daughter needed no consoling. Her anger was fierce. She made us swear never to reveal his name to anyone. I have never let his name pass my lips and here was her child, almost an adult, craving the information withheld from her.

"I'll tell my child about him when I know the time is right," Brenda had told us all.

Brenda never really bonded with her daughter. Any attempts by me urging her to spend more time with Lucy were ignored.

"She'll grow up so quickly," I would say to her. *"The baby years will be gone before you know it."*

The only response was a cursory glance at her child and a polite enquiry as to her development.

"Let me know if she requires anything."

Young Lucy wanted for nothing; she had all the material comforts available. Brenda spent lavishly on her child who was too young to be affected by her mother's lack of interest. I don't doubt she loves her daughter, but the lack of warmth!.

Lucy called me "mama", the name she still uses to this day. It was the first word she spoke. Her mother dutifully attended school events and was fawned over by staff, who felt privileged to have the daughter of a prominent member of the community attend their school. They never failed to mention Lucy's musical talent. Brenda once told on her return from such a meeting;

"Lucy has a bright future ahead of her in the musical world," commented one tutor. *"One that we are privileged to nurture."*

She would acknowledge the remark with a wry smile, saying, "Hmm, we'll see."

Brenda showed interest in Lucy's work for a time but never praised her. It was as if she didn't know how to express love.

When Lucy's music teacher first alerted her to the incredible talent of her child, Brenda threw dollars at providing the best instruments, set up a music room at home and employed Ken Farmer as her mentor. The man was in raptures at Lucy's ability to handle her cello and the ease with which she mastered the pianoforte. He felt his prodigy could skilfully handle any musical instrument that came her way.

Molly wiped a tear from her eye and continued with her thoughts:

And here we are, mother and daughter at loggerheads, not for the first time, and me, piggy-in-the-middle. As much as I'd like to shake sense into Brenda, I can't get involved. Her only child is moving further from her emotionally. I wish she would see how talented her child is, but she won't hear tell of Lucy following her musical dream. The kid hates the idea of a business career. It will all end in tears, I can see it coming, as sure as my name's Molly Kelly. To crown it all, the child wants to know about her father. I knew that would happen before too long. Her mother needs to tell her. Lucy has a right to know... but then... that's just my opinion...

Nora, returning home from a shopping expedition, found her mother attacking her chores with a fury, which she knew signalled trouble.

"What's wrong, mom?" she said, hugging the older woman.

"Oh, the usual! Lucy's upset and I've made things worse. She asked me who her father was and, of course, I couldn't reveal that now, could I?"

"No, mom, you're right. We made a promise and we have to keep to it, whether we like it or not. Where is Lucy?"

"She took off to her music room. Best leave her alone for a bit. She calms down once she picks up that cello. I don't think she'll come down for supper; you can take something up and she'll talk to you."

Nora, using the pretext of wanting to show Lucy her purchases, chatted with the distressed child until calmness was restored.

"Wish you were my real sister," said Lucy as she ate supper in her room, with Nora fussing around her, "and your mom was my mom. I hate my mother at times."

"Lucy, you will always be like my real sister and we will be friends for life. You're so lucky that your mother is rich; you'll want for nothing. I'll always be an employee and have to work for a living."

"I would trade places with you any day, Nora. I won't ever call her anything but 'mother', never mom. At times I think she doesn't even like me; she has little time to spare from that damn business…"

Nora became silent, knowing how right Lucy was. Later that evening, she sat in silence in her apartment, thinking how lucky she was to be so loved.

Sure, Lucy has everything she will ever need materially, her financial future is secure, but I hate to see her so sad, crying out for her mother to acknowledge her talent, to acknowledge her existence even.

Her thoughts drifted to when Lucy was born, enriching the Mears household, and she, Nora, becoming an honorary elder sister to the cute baby, helping with her early care, revelling in her development and conscious that the child's mother spent less and less time with her daughter, relinquishing more and more care to the staff.

"Let me know if she needs anything," was the usual utterance, as she rushed off to yet another meeting.

Too busy to care, missed the special moments, thought Nora as she remembered the precise moment when she and Brenda ceased being close friends and became employee and employer.

It was not long after Brenda had graduated from Cornell and began working with her father that she dropped me as a friend. We'd been brought up almost like sisters, best friends who played, laughed, shared secrets, dreamed dreams and promised to be friends forever. Thursday was our movie night... we would meet in town, eat dinner and head for the latest movie.

"Meet you as usual then?" I asked as I worked the breakfast room.

"Sorry, Nora, I've been thinking. Now that I'm involved in Father's firm and you are, in fact, an employee of mine, we should end our friendship. It would only lead to problems. I expect to be busier now. Could you clear these plates, please?" she concluded as she left the room, barely giving me a glance.

I felt slighted, and to say I was upset was putting it mildly. I felt like my ego had been destroyed in a second. Chores that day seemed endless. I couldn't wait to retreat to my room and let rip my anger and sorrow. Mom heard me crying.

"Honey, what's happened? Are you sick?"

I told her of my encounter with Brenda.

"Mom, I felt so small, like she'd slapped my face. Do our years of friendship count for nothing? She's a bitch. She thinks of no one but herself."

"We have to face it, we've been put in our places, both of us; looks like our relationship has changed now that she's working for the firm."

"You too, mom? Has she snubbed you?"

"Yeah, didn't want to say anything, but I was reminded we were employees, first and foremost."

CHAPTER 31

Having consoled her daughter, Molly returned to her chores and her own thoughts.

What I didn't tell my daughter was that our accommodation would no longer be free.

"*You have been cosseted enough over the years. It's time to pull your weight around here,*" said Brenda sharply.

Pull my weight! *I thought. I almost exploded with anger; I'd given a hundred percent to this family. I kept my lips sealed, my thoughts to myself. True, Brenda was always wilful, but never spiteful. I simply said, "Yes, ma'am," and continued with my chores.*

Life continued, with Nora and me attending to chores with a heavy heart. Calmness descended; we saw little of either Simon or Brenda as they worked ceaselessly to build their empire. That is, until one day a furious Brenda hollered for us to come to the kitchen where Simon, a pained expression on his face, sat beside his daughter.

"*I'm pregnant, and before you even think of offering any congratulations, don't bother. My lover, my esteemed politician whose aim is to serve his country, has dropped me. He doesn't want a kid interfering with his plans. He threw money at me and told me to get rid of it. What I have to say to you is never, ever reveal to anyone the name of my child's father.*"

My instinct was to take her in my arms as I used to do when she was upset, but that would not have been appreciated. I looked across at her father, a broken man, who seemed to have shrunk into himself. I hadn't noticed until then how ill he looked and a thought struck me... Oh God, he's really sick. Nora and I swore allegiance to her, assured our boss, as we had now come to think of her, that we would keep her secret.

"After all," I couldn't resist saying, "we have been loyal to you all your life."

The irony was lost to her.

"My father and I have a request to ask. Will you help with the care of the baby?"

"Of course we will. It will be good to have a young 'un around the place again."

She stormed out of the room without a glance at us, giving the impression that this was everyone else's fault but hers. Simon remained seated.

"Molly, Nora." He beckoned us to sit closer. "Forgive my daughter's attitude please. I know she's changed towards you, and you, of all people, don't deserve it. I have tried to get her to loosen up, but she's gotten a hard shell around her over the years and this pregnancy will make her even more difficult to live with. I blame myself for bringing her into the firm too soon. It's gone to her head completely and I'm not strong enough to fight her. She is brusque with my staff and I fear they will dislike her. You both need to know, I have terminal cancer, they say twenty-four months or so..."

His voice trailed off... I sensed underlying fear, poor man.

Simon wanted to talk more; we sat with him for over an hour drinking tea, until tiredness drove him to retire for the night. As he left the room he turned to me.

"Molly, please don't abandon my difficult daughter

*when I'm gone. I know she's fickle, but she'll need you
both, even if she won't admit it. I told her only yesterday
about my prognosis, then she dropped her own bombshell.
In a sense I'm pleased, as she will have the little one to focus
on when I'm no longer here."*

*With that, he shuffled off to bed; only then did I see
how thin he was... how sick.*

*The next few months passed quickly, luring me into a
sense of serenity. Simon handed over most of the running
of the firm to his daughter, while retaining overall control,
but becoming weaker as the weeks passed. Medical
assistants were employed to attend to his needs. The only
real dealings I had with him was to tempt him to eat by
producing some of his favourite meals. Brenda's pregnancy
proceeded normally and she continued with her business
ventures as usual.*

"I'm not ill," she would retort when it was suggested
she rest more.

Her daughter was delivered safely. Within a short
period, the new mother returned to work with renewed
vigour, as if she found childbirth a disruption to her busy
life. Simon rejoiced in the birth of his tiny granddaughter,
enjoyed many hours with the beautiful baby, conscious of
the fact that her care was more and more in the hands of
his household staff and that his own time with her was
now limited.

Molly, seated in her own apartment, knitted furiously
as if to vent her feelings on the garment, as she recalled
meeting Brenda's associates for the first time.

*One day, I was instructed to prepare a dinner party for
seven people. Brenda had, with her father's blessing,
gathered together her own specially selected team of trusted
associates and wished to introduce them to him during a*

bonding session. It was the first time I had met Myra Hill. I thought her a haughty kind of person; those cold eyes that never made direct contact with me as I served the meal gave me the shivers. She'll do well with Brenda, *I thought. Two of a kind.*

These dinner parties became a regular occurrence over the next few months and years. The highlight of the evening was when Lucy was brought into the company to be admired and fussed over, before being removed to the sanctuary of her nursery. Bob Lees and his partner Justin Palmer showed genuine interest, making all the right noises at the delightful child, unlike the aloof Myra and, to a degree, the Scotts. Olivia gave her a cursory glance; "sweet kid" was about as much as she could summon from those overly painted lips, while her husband, Ron, smiled dutifully as the adoring mother looked on.

Simon Mears' death had a shattering effect on his daughter, who had approached his illness with denial, making the final event more traumatic for her. It was the first time in many years that she had come to me in tears, seeking comfort.

"Oh Molly, what am I going to do without him? My dad! He told me how ill he was and I wanted to get him the best specialists, fly them in if necessary. God, we could well afford it, but he knew nothing could be done and did not want any more intrusive treatment. He just wished what time he had left to have some quality. He loved his little granddaughter and wanted to spend hours with her. Oh, Molly!"

As she sobbed in my arms, tension subsided in her shaking body. Finally, she became more composed and immersed herself into the funeral arrangements. Almost with undue haste, she returned to work. That did not surprise me.

The years flew or so it seemed to me, and young Lucy grew to be a delightful child who spent most of her time with me in the kitchen, chattering non-stop, confiding in me or following Nora around as she worked her chores. We adored each other.

Molly Kelly, *I chided to myself.* You won't get supper ready sitting around reminiscing or worrying about madam upstairs.

Madam, as Molly privately referred to her employer, sat in her office poring over the latest sales figures. Her recent spat with Lucy had had an unnerving effect on her. Normally she ignored her daughter's outbursts, but, this time, Lucy's plea touched a nerve in the normally resolute woman.

'*I'll make a point of taking time out with her to discuss her future and persuade her to come around to my way of thinking. I can still encourage her to continue learning with Ken Farmer; after all, I've spent a load of dollars equipping her music room. Granted, she plays beautifully, but come on… music as a career…?*'

Returning home that evening, Brenda looked for her daughter only to be reminded by Nora that she was staying over with Abigail.

"Slipped my mind. I'll speak to her tomorrow. By the way, how did it go at the dentist?"

"Good, thanks, the tooth was extracted and I'm fine now."

Nora thought that was about the longest conversation the two of them had had in months.

CHAPTER 32

Near the cabin in Montana, an elderly man sat listening to the radio report. His wife commented on a news item.

"Poor kid, that Lucy Mears. I wonder if she is still alive. Her folks must be frantic with worry."

"Yeah, strange business; no ransom demand and her mom's rich; strange indeed. Honey, I'd best get to the cabin, been asked to have it ready for tomorrow. Beats me why anyone would want to travel in this weather. It's the worst winter we've had in many years."

For a small payment, Gus and Ellie Stiller had looked after the cabin for several years, preparing it when required for visitors. It was easy enough for them to keep it stocked with groceries and logs. They seldom saw anyone occupy it and had clear instructions never to disturb the occupants. The couple led a quiet life, but in their youth they enjoyed all that Montana had to offer. Both were excellent skiers. Gus had helped with dog sled treks, while Ellie was involved in festival events.

"Who's coming this time?"

"I've been told it's some writer who wants peace and quiet to finish a book, been told not to disturb."

"Best get going before it gets dark then… mind the icy path."

The following evening Gus studied the menacing storm.

"Hey, Ellie, over there. Some kind of a vehicle on the

track near the cabin… looks like it's been abandoned. I'm going to have me a look-see."

Returning home, he told of his findings.

"Big campervan, New York plates… has a burst tyre, it won't be going nowhere for a while. Strange though, I'm sure I saw three sets of footprints… hard to tell though in the snow."

Next morning, Ellie stood by her kitchen window, binoculars focused across towards the cabin.

"Look, honey," she called to her sleepy husband. "I'm sure as hell certain I saw a young girl look out that window."

She handed the binoculars to her husband, who adjusted them and studied the cabin for some time, before commenting.

"Who would have a kid up here in this weather? Except…"

"You thinking' what I'm thinking'…? Could that be that missing kid? Hey, don't expect it is, miles from her home. Honey, I'd never forgive myself if I ignored this and then heard something awful had happened to any kid. Could be quite innocent, but, hell, I'm gonna call the police. Damn! No signal and I ain't driving to Polson. We'll just keep an eye open, see what transpires over the next few days. The kid's moving from window to window, but she didn't see me."

***

Superintendent Benson took a call from a colleague in Montana.

"Sir, we've had a call from a member of the public who thinks he might have located your missing kid in Montana.

Unfortunately, the weather here played havoc with signals, the call has only just reached me."

He proceeded to relay what Gus Stiller had told him.

"It may be a false sighting, but we sent some officers to the area. It was hellish difficult for them to reach it, but the cabin in question was empty. There were signs of recent occupancy. My team swept the place for prints, they are en route to your lab. I sent a chopper out to have a look around but had to recall it due to weather, but I've alerted other states to look for a large campervan with New York plates... with instructions not to impound it, but to watch where it finally stops. Hey, and I made some more enquiries. You will be interested in this info."

Benson was horrified to hear who owned the cabin.

"Well, I'll be damned... I'll get a team from N.Y. to visit the owner in question. Much appreciated, Officer. We have had several false sightings, but we check them all. This might just be the one!"

Meanwhile, a garage owner at Wisconsin, an elderly, sprightly man, contacted local police when he became suspicious of a customer who had brought his vehicle for repair. He regaled his memory of the event.

"It was some weeks ago now," he mused. "A guy drove in with a top-of-the-range campervan, said the engine was kind of dragging a bit and asked if I could have a look at it. It took me a couple of hours to sort out. He insisted on sticking around. I told him there was a coffee shop nearby where he would be out of the weather, but he wanted to stay and watch. I thought it kind of odd, but, what the heck, he was paying me to do the work and in wintertime I take all I can get. He didn't speak much. I guess he was foreign, Polish, maybe. I asked what he was doing driving such a vehicle in this hellish weather, but he was a bit reluctant to make conversation... said something about delivering it to a friend. Anyhow, I fixed the van and he took off. I noticed the plates, have it written here, got to keep good records, you know... New York plates, they were. Couple of days later I sees the guy driving past the garage. I waved over, but he seemed to ignore me... maybe he was concentrating on the road. Conditions weren't too good... now, the odd thing... I was sure I saw a kid, a young girl, look out from behind a window screen. Hey, it was just a glimpse... never thought much about it, just thought it odd to have a kid out of school and travelling along dangerous roads... wasn't till weeks later when I saw something on TV about a missing kid, I remembered the incident and called you guys. Hope I've not wasted your time or left it way too late."

"No way, sir, have you done that. In fact, you might just have given us valuable information. We are grateful for your observations. Someone will be in touch later; meanwhile, take this number, it will get you straight to the detective leading the enquiry, should you remember anything else, however small."

CHAPTER 33

Unaware of the melee surrounding them, Lucy and her companions left the cabin and continued their long journey, retracing their route. Due to her agitated state, Zelda had given her a mild sedative, which lulled the girl to sleep in the now very familiar campervan.

***

After a difficult journey, Lucy, free from sedation for several days, became more aware of her plight. She was extremely weary from travel and was relieved to hear Zelda proclaim, "Ten more minutes, Lucy, and all will be made clear to you. We have arrived."

The campervan turned into a driveway, which curved through an avenue of trees, coming to a halt in front of a large colonial-style house. An old sleepy dog stretched, raised itself up from its comfortable position and, tail wagging, approached the visitors. Zelda, first out, patted the dog, which snuggled up to her, enjoying being reunited with a familiar face.

"Hey there, Bud."

Kristof helped Lucy down from her prison for the last time and escorted her to the front door, which opened to reveal a man standing there awaiting their arrival.

"George!" hollered Lucy as she threw herself into his arms and succumbed to pent-up emotions suppressed for so long. She cried in his arms as the floodgates opened, tears flowing like an unstoppable tap. Lucy tried to speak; only sobs came out.

"Hush, Lucy, everything will be explained to you now. There's someone who wants to meet you. You'd best go freshen up first."

George hugged the weeping child until her sobs began to ease. He looked gaunt and pale, the past months having transformed him from a healthy robust man to a shadow of his former self. His eyes were red with constant weeping. He visibly relaxed as he held Lucy, knowing that soon their ordeal would be over.

"Zelda will take you to your room and stay with you until you are sent for. Don't worry, honey, everything will be fine and you'll soon be home. You've no idea how pleased I am to see you. We have so much to talk about and explain, but now freshen up. It will help you feel better."

Zelda, arm around the whimpering child, led her through an exquisite entrance hall: a circular area, ornately decorated with silk and gold leaf wall hangings. A few tasteful Chippendale pieces set between statuettes mounted on Doric pillars set a tone of elegance and wealth. She led the girl up an elaborate Mediterranean-style staircase to the first floor into a tastefully furnished bedroom, which Zelda stated had been decorated expressly for her stay.

"Who lives here? Whose house is this? Why am I here? I want to call Mama."

"Soon, child, soon," said Zelda, leading the child to where a set of designer clothes was spread out for her approval.

"The shower room is in there. Go freshen up and change clothes."

When Lucy reappeared, she seemed calmer, accepting her fate with a hope that she would soon be freed from this nightmare.

A tray of tempting food was set on a little table by the bay window affording stunning views over manicured gardens. Lucy ate, not from hunger but from habit. Zelda fussed about, humming to herself, relieved to have come to the end of a journey that had been undertaken in difficult circumstances. A knock came at the door and Zelda was instructed to escort the young guest to the master suite.

"Lucy, dragi dijete, baby, come with me to meet my boss."

Zelda led Lucy to a room in another wing of the house. She kept her arm around the shaking girl for comfort. Lucy took the room in at a glance; her mouth opened in amazement.

"My cello! My cello!" she cried as she spotted the instrument by the window recess. She almost ran to it but was halted by a soft, almost inaudible voice coming from an enormous bed.

"Not yet, child, be patient. Come here."

Lucy had been unaware of anyone in the bed, so enthralled was she to be reunited with her cello.

"Come over here, my dear. Oh my beloved Francesca!"

"No, you're mistaken, my name is Lucy Mears. I'm not your Francesca and I demand to go home. I don't know you or your Francesca."

Lucy had never seen anyone so thin, so skeletal, and so close to death. The woman in the bed appeared dwarfed by pillows and fine bedcovers, which encased her small, pathetic frame.

"I know who you are, my dear. Please excuse a

confused old lady. Come, sit by my bed while I explain everything to you. I am your great-aunt. I am Anna. Your grandmother whom you never knew was my darling baby sister, my Francesca, my dear, only sister, cruelly taken from me by your hateful mother."

"But my mother is not hateful, well, she's—"

"Ssh, child, I've not much time left, humour an old lady and listen to my ramblings. I reared Francesca when our parents died together in a selfish manner; I won't go into that, and you are too young. We were devoted to each other. She was beautiful; you are so like her, my dear, so similar you almost took my breath away when you came into the room, so like my darling Francesca."

The old woman coughed, spluttered and gasped for breath. A nurse, whom Lucy hadn't noticed, came across from the opposite side of the room to administer medication to her patient.

"You must rest, Anna," implored the nurse.

"Later, Rita, later. I'll have plenty of time to rest when I'm gone." The withered old lady attempted a laugh.

"Yes, my dear, my Francesca was beautiful. She fell in love with your grandfather Simon. What a handsome couple they made! What fun we had planning the wedding; no expense was spared. We were wealthy, Francesca and I, your grandfather too. Only the best was good enough for their wedding; 'the society wedding of the year,' reported the papers."

Rita came forward to see to her patient who halted her with a wave of her bony hand.

"My heart burst with pride to see them so happy together, so made for each other, so in love."

She fumbled in a drawer, but too weak to open it she asked Lucy to retrieve a picture for her.

"These are your grandparents, my dear. I want you to have it."

Lucy looked at the picture and inhaled deeply.

"That could be me!" she gasped.

"Yes, my dear, so alike, so beautiful! She was musical too, like you, she loved her piano. I keep it here with me where I can imagine her sitting playing to me."

Lucy looked in the direction Anna pointed. There at the other end of the room was a beautiful Steinway baby grand.

"You may touch it, dear."

Lucy looked at Zelda for confirmation. Zelda nodded, saying, "Go ahead, Lucy, play for us."

Lucy fingered the baby grand, caressing it lovingly, opened the lid and tapped the keys.

"Perfectly tuned," she said. "It's a beautiful instrument. I have one at home, but this is awesome."

"Why don't you play for me? There's music on the table."

While Lucy looked through the music, Anna tried to raise herself up in bed to allow a better view. Zelda helped Nurse Rita lift the frail lady as tenderly as they could, pain etched on the patient's face.

Lucy chose to play *Music of the Night* from one of her favourite modern composers.

Soon she was lost in the music, the past weeks temporarily forgotten as her nimble fingers moved skilfully and expertly over the keys. A calmness, not experienced for some time, filled the room. Her little audience was enthralled. Not a sound was heard save that of the shallow breathing of the sick lady. Zelda, never having heard Lucy play, wiped tears from her eyes as she listened to the child who had shared her life for the past months and whom she had grown fond of bring the instrument to life. Lucy came to the end of the piece, closed the lid and sat quietly for a few minutes, before turning round to her relative whose eyes were filled with tears. The child approached her aunt, took hold of her hand, looked into her sad eyes and, in spite of misgivings, bent forward and kissed her forehead. Rita gave her patient a few sips of water, dried the tears from the sunken cheeks and suggested Anna rest a while.

"I have so much more to explain to the dear child," she said, "and so little time to do it, but I do feel tired. Lucy, my little one, go with Zelda, have dinner and a restful night. We will talk tomorrow."

With that, the old lady nodded off.

Zelda, quiet and more composed than she had been for some time, led Lucy from the sickroom, downstairs to a comfortable dining room where they were serving an evening meal. They ate in silence.

After the meal, Lucy spoke out. "When can I call Mama?"

"As soon as your aunt gives permission. There is so much she has to tell you. You know she is dying, don't you?"

"Yeah, but I've never seen anyone so ill before, it doesn't frighten me. Where is George? I haven't seen him since I arrived; he can take me home. I need to talk with him."

"He and Kristof have an errand to do for your aunt; he will return soon."

Back in her room, Zelda assured Lucy she would sleep nearby.

"I have been instructed to lock you in, my dragi dijete; no harm will come to you."

They could not allow Lucy freedom to roam, partly

because she could find herself totally lost in the vast building, but more importantly, she could come across one of the many phones. Lucy spent a restless night, going over everything that she had learned since coming to this house and eventually fell asleep, emotionally drained. Zelda, carrying a breakfast tray, wakened her.

"It is such a pleasant day to walk in the garden. We shall take a stroll when you are ready. Wrap up well."

Lucy marvelled at the peaceful setting of the stunning gardens, the lily pond, the summerhouse covered in snow and the spectacular views beyond.

"My aunt must be very rich, richer than my mother. I've only seen places like this in the movies."

"She is extremely wealthy, but you know, dragi, money does not always bring happiness."

Bud, the old dog, meandered after them, stopping often to sniff the air, have his ears rubbed and amble on with his companions. Zelda showed her young charge around the vast estate, until summoned indoors. Returning to the warmth of the house, Lucy was once more called to her great-aunt's suite to learn more of the reason behind her captivity.

CHAPTER 34

"Good morning, Lucy. I trust you slept well."

Lucy approached her relative, gave her a peck on the cheek and waited to hear more from the elderly lady who appeared marginally brighter than the previous evening.

"I shall continue. You deserve an explanation. After the wedding the newlyweds headed off for a tour of European cities. Francesca sent copious letters from various places she visited: Rome, London, Paris, Venice, Florence, her favourite being Paris. She adored strolling along the South Bank, cruising on the Seine; the view from the Eiffel tower amazed her. She adored everything French and vowed to return there someday. They settled down to married life. Francesca and I visited each other when we could. Such happy times! Then she announced her news. She was pregnant; such joy for them! They decorated the nursery wing, refused all idea of employing a nanny, preferring instead to take on the care of their little one themselves. What plans they had! Your grandfather began advertising for a new housekeeper. Sally, who had been with him for as long as he could remember, wished to retire to go live with her niece in Florida."

Anna struggled for breath, had some more medication from the attentive Rita and insisted on continuing with her story.

"I owe it to the child," she told her nurse. "It is a fact of life, Lucy, that when one is so happy, something always comes along to destroy it."

The old lady closed her eyes as if the memory of what she was about to say pained her.

"And so it happened. Our idyllic life was shattered when Francesca died giving birth to her longed-for baby girl. Sadness cast a deep, dark shadow over your grandfather; nothing, not even his little daughter, could lift his spirits. He struggled to cope. Sally did her best, but she was too old to care for a young baby with all the attention it needed day and night. The strain was too much for her and I was sent for. It was a hard visit, to enter the home that had once been full of laughter and carefree frivolity, to a place that no longer held any pleasure for me. I was filled with such disquiet; for me, the house had become a mausoleum. My poor, dear Francesca, how I missed her. I wandered from room to room, stopping to remember how happy she had been. I could almost hear her laughter as she attempted to learn from Sally how to cook a special meal for her adoring husband and her sweet singing as she helped with chores, making her home into a little palace. When she sat at her piano, she enthralled Simon and me with the beauty of her playing; she was totally transformed from a frivolous, love-struck young lady to a serene, talented musician."

At that, the sick old lady convulsed in tears and Zelda removed Lucy to allow the patient some privacy.

"She will send for you later," intimated Rita.

Lucy sat by the window of her bedroom with Bud perched on her lap. She chatted quietly to the placid dog as she waited for someone to send for her. It was several hours before a pensive and subdued Lucy was recalled.

"I stayed with your grandfather and the baby Brenda for about four months," continued her aunt. "A strange feeling came over me, one that I cannot to this day explain."

Struggling for breath, Anna insisted on continuing with her account.

"I looked at that tiny helpless infant and felt nothing but resentment. I stood at the foot of her crib, sobbing for my dear Francesca and spoke to the child, as if it could understand.

"'You are only alive because my sister gave her life for you. Why didn't the doctors save her and let you die? She could have tried later for another child.'

"I was bereft. The longer I stayed in that house the more solemn I became, to the point of hatred for the baby and determined to have justice for Francesca. I had to leave. I intimated my intentions to your grandfather and only agreed to stay until suitable help could be found to replace Sally. And so I continued for a short time to care for Brenda, not with any love, but with hatred in my heart. It was a great relief to me when your grandfather introduced his new help, an Irish-American lady, Molly, who had a young daughter of her own."

Anna struggled to speak; Nurse Rita insisted she must rest, so yet again Lucy was escorted from the sickroom. With so much to digest, Lucy sat once more at the window seat in her room, looking out over the garden and pondering what had been revealed to her. Zelda, sensing she wanted to be alone, left her there while never straying far from her charge's room. Old Bud wandered in, ready for a walk with his new friend.

"Ok, Bud. Let's walk!"

Wrapped up well, the trio took a walk in the garden. Lucy spoke to Zelda.

"It is so unfair to blame my mother for Francesca's death. That's what this is all about, isn't it? Revenge."

"Grief takes many forms, my dear; everyone copes

differently, some people accept loss better than others and move on with their lives, while others take longer. Some, like your great-aunt, cannot let go of hurt. It eats into the core of their being, distorting and projecting the blame on to someone or something else. In blaming your innocent mother, she channelled her grief into extracting revenge, as if in doing so she would be free from emotional pain. Her whole life was poisoned by hatred that she sought revenge. That was how she saw it. Such a sad way to live. I don't expect she had one happy day throughout her life after Francesca's death."

"Francesca looked beautiful. To think I've never seen a picture of her until now. My mother has never once mentioned her to me, my own grandmother, but she's not that kind of mother who would talk of such things. I want to leave this hateful place, Zelda! Please let me call Mama; she will send someone for me immediately. Please, call Mama."

Zelda simply shook her head, wishing she could help the distraught child, but her hands were tied. She did not explain to Lucy why this had to be. They were summoned once more to Anna's room.

"I don't want to go there. I hate her and I don't care how sick she is."

Comforting the girl, Zelda implored her to hear her aunt out and then the ordeal would finally be over for her. Zelda knew Anna could be ruthless, even in these last days of her life. Anna, weakening by the minute, was becoming more difficult to hear and called Lucy to sit closer. Despite her apprehension, Lucy did as bidden, anxious to draw this chapter of her life to a close.

"I sense your animosity towards me, my dear child, and I do not blame you. I have unashamedly used you to make someone pay for my loss. I immersed myself in my work in antiques but never found peace. I filled this house with some exquisite pieces as if to compensate for other losses. And so, I decided I had to avenge Francesca's death the only way I knew: by making Brenda experience loss of someone beloved to her.

"I kept track of her movements, followed her career and heard of your birth. I felt my sister's loss even more as she was deprived of seeing her granddaughter and you, of course, from having what would have been the most wonderful grandmother to guide you in life. I followed your life too, heard of your musical talent and was determined to hear you play. When in Chicago, I heard your school orchestra was putting on a performance. I stayed on a few days more. I took my place at the back of the hall and was entranced when you stepped out to play a piece from Taube. I slipped away before the intermission, my heart beating fast as I saw the re-incarnation of my darling Francesca. I decided then to make Brenda Mears suffer a similar, albeit temporary loss of her only child."

Lucy could no longer contain her emotions.

"How cruel! My mother did you no wrong; she was only a helpless baby and she will be ill with worry about me. You are a sad old woman. I won't sit here any longer listening to your spiteful words."

With that, Lucy ran from the room, wishing to put as much distance between herself and her relative. She lay on her bed sobbing until she could cry no more. Her body was racked by pain from all the emotion. She fell asleep fully clothed. Zelda found her there, covered her with a comforter and left the child to escape from her misery through sleep.

Zelda was summoned to Anna's room. The patient was

noticeably weakened by the strain of her confession and the reaction of her niece, her voice barely audible now. Zelda came close to her employer, straining to hear what she had to say.

"Zelda, give this letter to the girl. I wrote it to be left for her should I not live long enough to meet her. What I have already told her is written here, and much more. Give this to her. She need not see me again if she so wishes. I have wronged the girl. I see that now. I was too focused on her mother to truly think of what I was putting such a young child through. She must hate me."

***

Next morning, having picked at her breakfast, Lucy's mood had not lifted.

"Let me out of here, let me call Mama. Send for George. I want to go home right now."

Zelda shook her head despondently, handed Lucy the buff envelope, explained what it contained and left her to read it at leisure. Bud wandered in beside her as if sensing her pain, lay at her feet and looked at her with his sad eyes pleading with his new friend to emerge from her gloom.

"I don't want to read this, Bud. I just want to go home."

She sat quietly, patted the dog, fed him titbits from her breakfast tray and spoke to him as if he were human. Lucy sat with Bud as the snow turned to relentless rain, which pounded the window like the beating of her confused mind.

"No walk today, Bud," she said, patting the dog. "We will sit here and care for each other."

Bud wagged his tail as if in total agreement.

Lucy fingered the large envelope, pondering what to do. Eventually she opened it and read.

"This was written by me should I be too ill to speak to you or had already gone to my maker."

The girl skimmed over the pages she had heard her aunt speak of, reached where she had left off and began to read. Her hands trembled as she held the paper and Bud, through his doleful eyes, pleaded with her to be assured of his presence.

"After hearing you play, my determination to take you from your home became even more urgent. I had indeed been to Chicago, to see a cancer specialist. My prognosis was not good. I had an urgent plan in place to take you from that vile woman, with people ready to carry out my bidding, and so I made a call. George North was assigned to set things in motion when he knew the situation was right. He hated this assignment, but had no choice given the hold I had over him. You need not worry about that; just know that the people involved in your plight were reluctant players, all beholden to me. You were to be mildly sedated; George protested about this, to no avail.

"He was to deliver you to the care of a man called Dale Greer whose task was to escort you by bus from Halsted to Westwood and hand you over to a woman called Clara Blake in New York. After your overnight bus ride, you were to remain there with her for a few days.

"My little cabin in Montana is a special place. My dear sister and I visited each year and marvelled at the scenery. No matter how often we visited, the scenery enthralled us. We were there each May for the Bigfork Whitewater festival and gasped in awe as the competitors rode the rapids. We visited Wild Horse Island where we boated and swam. Winter, too, was a magical time there. We would sledge and ski, Francesca being the better skier by far. I so wanted you to share the scenery, the views over Flathead Lake, its magical atmosphere, so loved by your grandmother. I instructed your companions to remain there for some time, to rest up and for you to enjoy, if that was possible in your situation, the splendour of the region. By now I hoped your mother would be frantic with worry and, given her obscene wealth, expect a ransom demand. I do apologize for the long, tedious journey. My instructions were that no harm was to come to you. You were to have mild sedation so that you would relax and be unaware of the length of the journey. I would never harm you, dear granddaughter of my Francesca.

"I planned for you to be away from your mother for as long as possible to let her experience loss. I wanted you to be comfortable and cared for during your captivity. I knew Zelda and Kristof would care for you, protect you and keep you calm. My dear, you must have been distraught, but you were the only means I had of hurting Brenda Mears, the one person I blamed for the loss of my dear sister, Your temporary home had to be the best. I trust it was at least satisfactory.

"Once relaxed, you were to return here to visit me. George was ordered to have your cello with him. I wished him to be the first person you saw on arrival and your beautiful cello to be in a prominent position waiting to be reunited with its owner. I longed to hear you play my Francesca's Steinway, to hear it come to life again at the fingers of her grandchild, and to hear you play your cello. Such talent! Such a gift! Such genius!

"I am tired now; my body is shutting down, the cancer rampaging through this worn shell of a person. I beg you to forgive a foolish old lady who forced this captivity on you for her own selfish satisfaction. Letters from me, exonerating those forced to execute my wishes, are lodged with my lawyer. The law will deal with them as it sees fit, but I hope sympathy and understanding will prevail.

"As for you, dear child, arrangements are in place for you to fly home. Do not judge me too harshly; love makes people do crazy things. Do not hate me; instead, hate my actions. Now, dear little one, goodbye."

Lucy put the letter down, hugged Bud, found comfort in the wise old mutt and sobbed unrelentingly. Zelda, who had been pacing the corridor, joined the child in her room. Lucy, aware of her presence, threw herself into the arms of the woman she had come to know as a friend and continued weeping.

"I want to see my great-aunt."

"You shall, Lucy. Let's dry your eyes, compose yourself. We cannot let your aunt see how upset you are; she is so sick now and won't be with us much longer."

Zelda held Lucy by the hand and led her to Anna's bedroom for the last time. Nurse Rita sat by the old lady, holding her hand, and gently administered to her patient as life ebbed towards its close. Lucy came to her relative's side, held the wrinkled hand and kissed the clammy cheek. Anna's eyes fluttered, focused on the child and a spark of recognition lit the aged face.

"Lucy," whispered the rasping voice. "Play for me."

Lucy moved over to her cello, caressed her precious instrument, chose Taube's gentle nocturne for cello and began to play. The room fell silent, the occupants lost in the moment. Stillness and calm touched each soul. When the piece finished, Anna held her wrinkled arm out.

"Awesome, my dear! Awesome! Goodbye my little Francesca. Go home now… go call Mama."

CHAPTER 35

Kristof returned the campervan to the hire place from where he had picked it up, which now seemed to him an eternity ago. He waited as it was checked over for damage. The mechanic reported all was well and remarked, "High mileage noted... you been round the world or something, buddy?"

"Seemed like it," replied the exhausted man before being driven off by George.

※

Zelda led Lucy from the room. The pair walked together into the garden, Bud rambling beside them. They wiped tears from their eyes.

"She wasn't a bad person, Lucy; she just did a bad thing."

"Oh, when can I call Mama?"

"Kristof and George have a final assignment at the airfield. They have to arrange a flight to take us all to Chicago by private jet, which your aunt often chartered. It's on standby, waiting for word for us to leave. They will come by, pick us up and take us to the airfield. Then you can make that call."

"My cello! I mustn't forget it."

"You play beautifully, Lucy. Your aunt was fortunate to hear you play before she passed away."

Rita, red eyed, joined them in the garden and addressing Zelda, said, "Lucy should be filled in on some things before she goes."

Taking the child by the arm, she began. "You will be leaving here in a few hours. I have to stay and close up. The funeral arrangements are in place. Your aunt had everything organized. It's to be totally private, with just myself and her lawyer present."

"Where will you go, Rita?"

"Zelda, the house will be sold. Anna has made several bequeaths to people who have been working for her. I plan to go to England to stay for a time with my cousin, while I decide what to do. Before we leave, it's only right that Lucy hears our story."

For the next hour, Zelda and Rita between them explained the hold Anna had on them all.

"You too, Rita? She had something on you?" gasped Zelda. "I did not know that."

"I'm ashamed to say, yes. When I was nursing I did something I shouldn't have. I took drugs from the hospital. Anna was a patient there at the time and caught me helping myself. She had come along so quietly for some painkillers that I hadn't heard her."

"You stole drugs from a hospital?" asked a horrified Lucy.

"Yes, Lucy, I was desperate... you see, my father was very sick, he was in such pain. I'd used all our Medicare health insurance... he was so ill... I was desperate. I had been taking a few drugs at a time, altering records and seemed to be getting away with it until Anna caught me. She knew exactly what I was up to. I pleaded with her not to tell anyone. I needed the job and I needed the drugs. We came to an agreement that I would leave the hospital and come work for her as her private nurse when my father passed on. She knew then she had only a few years left and needed nursing care at home. In spite of the hold she had over me, we became friends.

"She confided in me, trusted me and I loved her for that. Lucy, it must be hard for you to understand the hold your aunt had over us all. I would have been imprisoned if she had reported me to the authorities and there was always that fear in me that she might renege on her promise to protect my actions. In the end, I was dismissed from my job for bad timekeeping. I had to stay home so often to tend to my father and was regularly turning in late. I'm not sure if they ever knew about the drugs. I feel deep down that Anna would never have reported me. I think she saw my plight as a way of procuring for herself a qualified medic for the last stages of her illness."

"And Kristof and I, we could have been deported," said Zelda, as she related to the stunned girl the events of life in Bosnia, leading to their arrival in America. Lucy wept as Zelda told of the carnage and destruction of her country.

"You lost your little baby?" wept Lucy.

"Sadly, yes, and I can't have any children now. Lucy, you will never know how caring for you helped me heal emotionally."

Rita spoke up. "Zelda, what you and Kristof didn't know was that you would not have been deported. Anna told me that humanitarian measures had been put in place to help people like yourselves settle in America. She withheld that information from you as she needed your continued fear in order to carry on with her wild idea. She forbade me to talk to you about it. I think she used me like her confessor to get things off her chest before she went to her maker."

The two hugged and sobbed in each other's arms, weeks of pent-up emotions released like a river in spate.

"That's some story, Zelda. Wow! You've been through so much. I just knew, when we talked in the cabin, that you were afraid of someone or something. But, George, how could Aunt Anna have anything on him? He lives in my house, he's so kind and loves Nora, and he'd do anything for her."

"That was his problem! He was ambitious for them both," continued Rita as she related Anna and George's connection with Barclay Jones and his sordid money-lending business. I never liked him at all, nor his buddy Alf. Another guy, Les, is a much nicer guy. They did various jobs for Anna. I kept well out of their way, but I knew they were dangerous, devious people to deal with. Your aunt was in complete control of them... she was a strong character. They needed her money and she needed their ruthlessness—"

Lucy butted in. "But surely Mother would have lent George money if he had asked."

"He was a proud man and would not ask for help and he suffered the consequences."

Rita filled Lucy in with the connection with Clara and Dale.

"They were victims too of the money-lending scam. They couldn't go to the authorities for fear of reprisals from the thugs. There was such a hold over them that Anna was able to ensnare them too. It was she who put up the money to fund the whole sorry business."

"So that's who took me on that long bus journey? Dale Greer? He rarely spoke, looked scared, and the lady I stayed with, she was kind but quiet too. I seemed to sleep a lot."

They sat in silence for a while, each deep in thought. Then Lucy remembered something.

"Bud! What about Bud? Who will care for him? Can we bring him home with us?"

Rita gently replied to the excitable girl. "No, Lucy. Bud is too old to travel; you can see how slow he is. Your aunt has arranged for him to go stay with her lawyer and his wife who have recently lost their dog and long to have another pet. The arrangement will work well. He will be well looked after."

"Oh Bud, I'll miss you!" said Lucy as she snuggled beside the aged animal.

George and Kristof arrived back, both looking exhausted. Lucy sat with George as he drank coffee. They spoke little; Lucy from confusion and George more from shame.

"I have one more thing to do, Lucy. I have to run some guys to the airfield, then we can all go home. I'm sorry about all this, honey, I truly am sorry."

George, with Alf in tow, met with Les and made arrangements at the airfield to hire the plane regularly used by Anna for her various exploits. As they completed the documentation, they were given the news that their usual plane was not available.

"Got something kind of similar," they were informed. "Not as big, but reliable like the Gulfstream."

Les, who was to pilot the plane, was anxious to have it checked out to ensure it would suit the purpose. He made a detailed inspection of the aircraft and declared it suitable.

"Why don't you and George go get coffee, Les," suggested Alf, "while I fuel up? We want this baby up to scratch and ready for take-off."

While George had coffee, Les excused himself to visit

the restroom. As arranged and with dollar signs in his eyes, he called Detective Harvey.

"I have flight information for you, sir, like you asked."

George arrived back at Anna's house, helped load the luggage and the treasured cello into the sedan. Lucy and George talked as they walked for the final time in the garden.

"Everything has been explained to me, George. Let's go home."

"Honey, I'm not sure if I'll be able to work for your mother. She won't want me anywhere near you and I might be arrested in spite of what your aunt said about giving letters to her lawyer to vindicate us."

George wiped a tear from his eye and continued to explain to Lucy.

"I've messed up and I'm just going to have to face the consequences, whatever they are. We'll leave it to the law. Poor Nora, we had such plans."

"She will understand when she hears about things. I'll make sure she does… and Mama too."

"If only, honey, if only."

Kristof called them over. "It's time to go. Let's get this young lady home where she belongs."

He hugged Lucy and handed her his mobile phone.

"Lucy, at last, you can go call Mama."

The only number she could remember took her straight through to her mother's private number.

CHAPTER 36

Brenda Mears, weary with fear for her daughter's safety, sat at home attempting to attend to some paperwork. She thought how fortunate she was to have such a staunch team to carry on in her absence, especially, she mused, when they too were suffering with her over Lucy's disappearance. She sobbed quietly, something she felt she had been doing every moment of every day.

Molly served a snack. "You must try to eat something, you're fading away; you can't help Lucy if you make yourself ill. Come on, just a bite or two."

Molly stayed there, encouraging, cajoling and being as supportive as she could. The strain was telling on her too. She worried about Nora, who had withdrawn into herself over the fate of her fiancé. She was proving to be of little use with the household chores.

"Molly, sit by me and have something to eat too."

The women sat in silence, words superfluous as human contact became more necessary than anything anyone could say. Molly studied her boss, her Brenda, and thought of how the years had changed the once sweet girl she had nurtured and loved into such a hard woman almost incapable of showing love to those who mattered. As they sat there, Brenda's phone rang. The two women froze; few people had access to that number and it seemed an eternity until Brenda managed to pick up.

"Mother, I'm coming home, tonight!" gulped a weeping, breathless Lucy.

"Lucy! Lucy!"

Molly held Brenda's hand as she listened to a garbled story unfold from the emotional girl.

"Take a breath, honey, slow down."

She listened intently, Molly catching some of the drama.

"What?" screamed Brenda. "Anna did this? My aunt Anna stole you from me?"

"There's so much to tell you. Anna died. I love you, Mother." Lucy took a breath and continued. "I just want to be back home, I can't wait, I'm so happy. George will bring me home…"

"George did this? He is with you? Put him on, honey."

Kristof gently took the phone from Lucy's hand.

"I am sorry, madam, but we have to go now. Our private flight will arrive at Chicago Midway late evening. Your daughter is well."

"Who are you?" screamed Brenda, but the call had ended.

Nora, alerted by the loud voices, joined the others.

"What's going on? Is it news of Lucy?"

"Yes, and George," sighed Molly, elation mixed with confusion.

Between them, Brenda and Molly related what they had gleaned from Lucy, interspersed with tears and hugs.

"But George? What's been happening? Oh God," wept Nora. "How could he be involved in all this misery?"

"We have to get to Midway tonight. Molly contact Myra; tell her and the others what has happened. We need to let Detective Harvey know… oh… I can't think straight."

At the headquarters of Mears Empire, Brenda's elated, trusted team cheered loudly, hugged each other and wiped away tears of euphoria.

"Thank God it will soon be over. Poor child!" wept the excitable Justin as he clung to his partner.

Detective Harvey, working in his office, took the call that he had so longed for and hoped would solve the dreadful crime and bring closure to so many people. With a grin on his delighted face, he almost ran into a junior officer as he rushed to his deputy's office to give her the news. Together they drove to Brenda Mears' home, where for the first time in many weeks the atmosphere was euphoric. There, Brenda related what she could remember of the call.

"Lucy was so excited! Someone, a foreign-sounding man, took the phone from me and spoke briefly. Oh, detectives, I can hardly believe it. Lucy is coming home!"

CHAPTER 37

Later that evening, a group of anxious people waiting in a private lounge at Midway International experienced an immense range of emotions: stress, euphoria, anxiety and excitement.

Detective Harvey reiterated details of what was to happen.

"Flight controllers will direct the plane to this area here," he began, pointing to a specified part of the airfield. "We have armed officers concealed, ready to move at my command. Officer Carr and I will board the plane with two armed officers. She will escort Lucy to you, Brenda. Lucy will be reunited with you and moved swiftly from the area to Mount Sinai Hospital to be checked over. It's going to be harrowing for you, but we are here for you. Detective Carr will be with you all the way. Armed officers will impound the aircraft and take custody of the people on board. As yet, we only know the identity of Lucy and George North. There are two other, unknown passengers, plus the pilot. We will bring this nightmare to a swift conclusion."

As time drew nearer for her reunion with her daughter, Brenda shook uncontrollably. Detective Carr held the scared woman close to her, shaking too as the drama that had coloured her life and her career for so long was nearing its end. Molly held Nora's trembling hand, the latter's mind in turmoil as to how her beloved George could possibly be involved in such a crime and pondered about his fate and their future.

✻✻✻

On board the plane no one spoke, each kept his or her thoughts to themselves. Lucy, weary but ecstatic at the thought of coming home, clutched her treasured cello, refusing to hand it over for safekeeping.

"I've been without it long enough," she told George when he suggested placing it in the hold.

Zelda and Kristof sat side by side, holding hands, their silence speaking for them. What thoughts and memories were stored in their hearts!

George appeared more agitated than the others. He suspected his life with Nora was over.

'*How could she ever trust me again?* he reflected. *Even if she took me back, would Molly accept me?*'

The fasten seatbelt light came on. Zelda reached over, secured Lucy's belt for her and gave her a reassuring hug.

"It won't be long now, dragi, until you are home."

Lucy looked out of the window and mouthed, "I'm coming home, Mama."

As the runway came in to view, two warning lights appeared on the instrument panel. Les, who had piloted the plane with his usual expertise and was about to begin his descent, knew immediately the significance of the lights.

"God, no!" he exclaimed.

✻✻✻

Fox 32 News was the first to report.

"A private plane crashed on approach to Chicago

Midway International. The plane left Teterboro airport en route for Chicago with five people on board, including the pilot and a child. At this stage, all are presumed dead. The aircraft was a private charter. The plane had an exceptional safety record. Early suggestions to the cause of the accident centre on a bird strike. No one on the ground was injured. Onlookers waiting in the private lounge witnessed the crash."

Fox later reported that there were no survivors. Airport authorities quickly discounted the bird strike theory and suspected sabotage. Among those waiting for the flight to arrive was Brenda Mears, mother of missing fifteen-year-old Lucy. Among the debris, investigators found the remains of a smashed cello.

Officers entering the gates of a palatial property in New York in order to speak to the owner had to give way to a funeral hearse exiting the premises.

***

ABOUT THE AUTHOR

Terry H. Watson is a retired, contented special needs teacher who has recently taken up writing.

Call Mama is her first novel inspired by impatience and curiosity while waiting for an author to complete the next book in a series. Why does it take so long to write a book? Now she knows!

Terry is currently working on a sequel to *Call Mama* called *Scamper's Find*, which will follow some of the characters to a new chapter in their lives. Terry has recently completed a collection of short stories, *A Tale or Two and a Few More*.

Terry lives in Scotland with her husband and a dining room overflowing with books and model boats.

Contact her on: terryhwatson@yahoo.co.uk